joie élève _ le plaisir affaiblit _ la joie rend fort. Cultivez
en vous le sens et l'amour de l'effort; c'est une part
essentielle de la dignité de l'homme et de son efficacité.
L'effort porte en lui-même sa récompense morale, avant de se
traduire par un profit matériel qui d'ailleurs arrive tôt ou tard
Lorsque vous aurez à faire choix d'un métier, gardez vous de la
double tentation du gain immédiat et du minimum de peine
Visez de préférence aux métiers de qualités qui exigent un long et
sérieux apprentissage, ceux-là même où notre main d'œu-
vre nationale accusait autrefois une supériorité incontestée
Lorsque vous aurez choisi votre carrière, sachez que vous aurez
le droit de prendre place parmi les élites C'est à elle que
revient le commandement, sur les seuls titres du travail
et du mérite.
Dans cette lutte sévère pour atteindre le rang que vos ca-
pacités vous assignent, réservez toujours une place aux vertus
sociales et civiques, à l'entraide au désintéressement à la
générosité x
La maxime égoïste qui fut trop souvent celle de vos de-
vanciers : Chacun pour toi et personne pour tous, est
absurde en elle même et désastreuse en ses conséquences.
Comprenez bien mes jeunes amis que cette individualité
dont nous nous vantions comme d'un privilège est l'o-
rigine des maux dont nous avons failli périr

WITH GRATITUDE to Fanny Krieger, who shared her story with me, and with admiration that her loving and generous spirit could not be stifled by the Nazi horror.

A Pocket
Full of Seeds

MARILYN SACHS

Illustrated by Ben Stahl

DOUBLEDAY & COMPANY, INC.
GARDEN CITY, NEW YORK

ISBN: 0-385-06091-2 Trade
0-385-06092-0 Prebound
Library of Congress Catalog Card Number 73–79708
Copyright © 1973 by Marilyn Sachs
All Rights Reserved
Printed in the United States of America
9 8 7 6 5 4 3 2

The broken dike, the levee washed away,
The good fields flooded and the cattle drowned,
Estranged and treacherous all the faithful ground,
And nothing left but floating disarray
Of tree and home uprooted,—was this the day
Man dropped upon his shadow without a sound
And died, having laboured well and having found
His burden heavier than a quilt of clay?
No, no. I saw him when the sun had set
In water, leaning on his single oar
Above his garden faintly glimmering yet . . .
There bulked the plough, here washed the updrifted
        weeds . . .
And scull across his roof and make for shore,
With twisted face and pocket full of seeds.

                    EDNA ST. VINCENT MILLAY

February 1944

M ADEMOISELLE LEGRAND called me heartless this afternoon.

After saying it, she waited for me to respond, but I said nothing. I do not want to argue with Mlle. Legrand. After all, she has taken me in and is protecting me from the Germans at some risk to herself, and I must be grateful for that. And then, Maman said, in the last message she sent me, that I should not talk back to grownups, and I am trying to do what she asked.

But it isn't easy. Mlle. Legrand is like a child, like I was in regard to Monsieur Bonnet. Expecting grief to be shown in such a way that those who are not feeling it will be able to recognize it. "Ah, look at poor Nicole! See how thin she is! How sad she looks! How she never laughs or plays with anyone! Poor thing! She is grieving for her family who were taken by the Germans."

I, too, back when I was still with my family, and did not understand, I thought M. Bonnet was heartless. Hadn't his wife died? Wasn't he separated from his children? How could he laugh?

Now I know that grief is not something you wear upon your face. It is inside you at night when you lie there in bed, listening to the country girls talking about their families. They know where their mothers and fathers are, and you do not. It is seeing the packages that come with a little piece of cheese or sausage or a warm scarf —and there are no packages for you. It is when the

3

mothers and fathers come to take their children home for the holidays or for Sunday, and their faces wrinkle up in smiles when they see their children. And there are no mother and father faces for you.

I miss them when I'm cold in bed at night under the thin, worn blanket, and when I'm hungry because there has not been enough to eat—and there is never enough to eat now. Most of all, I miss them when someone has attacked me, like Mlle. Legrand did this afternoon, and I have nobody to tell it to. Those times are the worst.

Huguette, in the bed next to me, reaches over, and pokes my arm. "Are you asleep, Nicole?"

"No."

"I have some licorice. Here, hold out your hand."

I hold out my hand, and she puts the licorice into it. It is only two small pieces, but I chew them slowly, moving them around in my mouth with my tongue before I swallow. Tonight I am so hungry, I almost believe I could eat tripe.

"I almost believe I could eat tripe," I say to Huguette. "I am so hungry."

"Not me," she says. Huguette's family lives on a farm out in the country near Culoz. Her cheeks are no longer as round and pink as they used to be but she is still the heaviest of all the girls in the dormitory.

"That is because you get more to eat than the rest of us," says Georgette, on the other side of Huguette. "But I don't think I will ever be able to eat tripe, no matter how hungry I am."

"Perhaps," I say, "it is because none of us is really starving."

4

"I am starving," Hélène moans from across the room. "All I ever think about is food."

"Yes," I say, "but we are not really starving because if we were, we would eat the tripe. When you are really starving you eat anything—worms, grass, shoes, people . . ."

"Ugh," Georgette says, "I would rather eat worms than tripe."

"Would you rather eat people than tripe?" asks Hélène.

"Certainly," Georgette says, "and when the time comes, I will start with Huguette. The rest of you are too bony."

"Oh, shut up," Huguette says, and all of us laugh. A little later when the others are sleeping, she reaches over, pokes my arm again and puts another piece of licorice into my hand.

She is more generous than the other girls in sharing her food. Perhaps because she gets more than anybody else. But after she has had all she wants, I am usually the first she will give extras to. It may be because I help her with her schoolwork, or it may be because she is sorry for me. Or feeling guilty. Like tonight.

But she was not to blame. It was the tripe. We had it for dinner today. We have it for dinner every Monday, and every Monday I am prepared. I carried a paper bag back with me from our classes to the dining room. Today was the dreariest of dreary days in a dreary month. Nothing but rain and sleet for days and days and days. The cold reached up under our skirts and down below our collars. It was in our nostrils, our ears, and behind our eyelids.

The dining room was so cold we had to keep our coats and hats on. We sat down at our places at the table, recited the grace and waited while the girls on kitchen duty that day began serving. You could smell it even before the large bowls were brought to each table.

Tripe smells like tripe. Once you have smelled it you can never mistake it for anything else.

I opened my paper bag and held it between my legs under the table.

The plate of tripe was before me. For a while the sight of it and the smell of it was enough to make me forget how hungry I was. I picked up a piece of it on my fork, and looked at the head of the table where Madame Chardin was seated. She was still busy dishing out the tripe. I moved my fork underneath the table, and quickly dropped the piece of tripe into the bag. Across the table from me, Hélène smiled and fluttered her eyelashes. There were at least three of us at the table holding paper bags between our legs.

Little Jeanne-Marie at the next table was crying as she did every Monday. Her teacher, Mme. Reynaud, was explaining how nourishing tripe was, and that Jeanne-Marie *must* eat it. *All of it!* And be grateful she wasn't one of the starving children in France who had nothing at all to eat. Poor Jeanne-Marie! If she were older, we could tell her about the bag trick, but she was too young, and we could not run the risk of exposure. There was no way of saving her.

My plate was empty. Mme. Chardin, looking around the table, nodded approvingly at me. Slowly I ate my piece of bread, and slowly I drank the bitter coffee.

Everything felt wet and damp that day. It seemed impossible to dry off. After classes, in the study hall, nobody could concentrate on homework. There was no heat. Our clothes were cold and clammy. You sat in your chair over the table, and felt the shivers radiating out in all directions from the back of your neck. And you were hungry.

"Listen to my teeth chattering," I said to Hélène.

"Mine are chattering louder," she said.

"No, mine are—and faster, too. Listen!"

Hélène and I had a teeth chattering contest. Marie was the judge. I won.

"I am so cold," moaned Huguette, "my fingers are numb even under my gloves, and my feet—I can hardly feel my feet."

"I know how to get warm," I said, shutting my book. "Everybody up—up—up!"

"What are we going to do?" asked Huguette. "It's colder standing up than sitting down."

"We're going to dance," I said. "Like the Americans. We are going to jitterbug. I can still remember the movies where they did it—like this—and this . . ."

I snapped my fingers and began jumping around, first on one foot and then on the other. I grabbed Marie around the waist, and we both jumped around together and went under each other's arms.

Hélène started to sing, and soon most of the other girls were dancing too. We turned and twisted and jiggled our hips. Huguette began laughing and her face turned red and her nose ran and she couldn't catch her breath but she kept on laughing.

"Here, look at me, look at me!" Marie said. She kicked her left foot way up above her head.

"Look at me, look at me!" Georgette yelled. She stood

on her head, balanced herself, and began walking upside down on her hands. Her skirt flopped down around her ears, and her underpants were full of holes.

I was dancing by myself now, around and around, twisting and twirling and stamping and warm, beautifully warm, and with my throat full of laughter.

I could hear the clapping and the singing, and I threw my head back and laughed.

I don't know when the clapping and singing ended. Because it was in the midst of one glorious twirl that I became aware of the other girls motionless, and in the midst of another one of Mlle. Legrand standing in the doorway.

"I cannot understand this display of levity," she said when I had become as motionless as the others. "Unless it means that you girls do not have enough homework to do. I will discuss this with your teachers, you may be sure of that. In the meantime, perhaps one of you will be good enough to explain your disgusting behavior."

Silence.

"Marie! You are the oldest, and I have always considered you dependable. Can you explain what happened here?"

"No, Mademoiselle."

"Georgette?"

"Mlle. Legrand, it was so cold. We were all cold and hungry . . . and we couldn't sit still without our teeth chattering and . . ."

"I see," said Mlle. Legrand. "You decided that you were too cold and hungry to do your work so you would just

make a lot of noise, and disturb anyone else who was trying to work."

"Oh, no, Mademoiselle. We weren't planning to disturb
anyone," said Huguette. "We just thought we would dance
to keep warm, and Nicole . . ."

"Yes? . . . and Nicole?"

Huguette turned toward me helplessly. Her face was
remorseful.

I finished the sentence for her. "I offered to teach them
how to jitterbug, Mademoiselle."

"Jitterbug?" Mlle. Legrand said, her eyebrows raised.
"What is that?"

"Jitterbug is the fast dancing the young people do in
the United States."

Mlle. Legrand said, "Nicole, the last person in the world
who should be dancing is you. What kind of feelings do
you have for your parents? For your sister? I am sure
that wherever they are, uncertain of your safety, and en-
during Heaven only knows what kind of suffering, I am
sure that they would never choose to dance. I believe you
must be heartless."

That was why Huguette was feeding me licorice tonight.

Soon she was asleep too. I have one small piece of
licorice left, and I put it under my pillow to save for tomorrow.

My mother comes to me first tonight. She sits on the
edge of my bed, and smiles at me, and strokes my hair.
"Why don't you eat your licorice?" she says.

"I am saving it for tomorrow," I tell her.

"Aren't you hungry now?"

"Yes, I am."

"Well then, eat it now."

I bite a piece out of my licorice, and my mother sits there, watching me.

"Maman," I tell her, "today Mlle. Legrand called me heartless, and she was wrong, but I didn't tell her so."

"I'm very proud of you," she says. "You are really growing up."

"I'm nearly fourteen, Maman."

"Yes, and when we are together again we will have to celebrate."

"Maman."

"Yes?"

"What is it like where you are? Do you have enough to eat? Are you warm enough? Are they mean to you?"

"We will manage," Maman says, "and so must you, and as soon as we can, we will all be together again."

"I know that, Maman, but sometimes I am very lonely, like now, because I know you're not here, and tomorrow I know you won't be here either."

"Think about when we will be together," Maman says. "Always think of that. That is what I am doing."

"And what I am doing too," says Papa. He is standing there next to Maman, smiling at me.

"And me too," says Jacqueline, and she climbs into bed with me. She is shivering so I hold her in my arms and kiss her and comfort her, just like I used to do when she was scared of something. After a while she stops shivering, and she curls up in my arms and says,

"Go ahead now, Nicole, and tell me one." Just like she used to do.

"Oh no, Jacqueline," I say, "not tonight. Why don't we just go to sleep."

"No!" She pushes me with her elbow, and says, "No! I want you to tell about me and Atlantis."

So I make up a story about her, how she was a princess in Atlantis. I have been telling her these stories for years, even before we lived with our parents. She loves to hear them but I always have to make sure that she is the princess and always wears a different color dress.

"Say what I wore."

"You wore a blue dress with a belt made of little silver bells."

"And on my head?"

"A crown made of silver with a ruby rose on each tip."

"And in my hand?"

"You held a golden scepter."

"Last time I had a bouquet of flowers."

"A scepter is very nice. It means you are the ruler, and nobody can do anything you don't like."

"I'd like a magic wand better."

"All right, then you can have a magic wand."

Before, I used to think Jacqueline was a nuisance when she woke me up, and I used to tell her so, too. But now when I feel her beginning to slip away, I beg her to stay. I promise to tell her lots of stories—as many as she wants. But she goes, and I am there alone, shivering in the darkness. So I eat my last piece of licorice, and go to sleep.

May 1938

I WAS EIGHT YEARS OLD when I came to live with my parents. Jacqueline was four. Before that my parents could not afford to keep us.

Both of them worked. They sold ladies' sweaters and blouses in the open-air marketplaces of the towns and villages around Aix-les-Bains where they lived. Each day, they went to a different place. On Monday it was Belley, Tuesday Annecy, Wednesday they remained in Aix-les-Bains, Thursday Rumilly or Bellegarde, Friday Annemasse, and Saturday Chambéry.

Each day they rose at dawn, and carried their heavy stock to the train. Each night they returned, carrying whatever had not been sold. They had a room for themselves in a boardinghouse, and they found a family a few miles outside of Aix-les-Bains who took care of my sister and me, and charged my parents very little.

This was M. and Mme. Durand. They were strict and very religious. We had to say our prayers every night, and go to church with them on Sunday. If we squirmed or wiggled too much, Mme. Durand would pinch our legs. But the food was good, only there was much more of it than we could eat. Mme. Durand had three boys, all rosy-cheeked and chubby. She thought Jacqueline and I were too skinny, and was always trying to fatten us up.

M. Durand sold cheeses, and breakfast, dinner, or supper there was always cheese—Brie or Tomme de Savoie,

Roblochon, Gruyère, or Camembert. Mme. Durand had cheese in the pantry at all times. The children could have as much as they wanted of that cheese. But downstairs, M. Durand kept the cheeses that he was going to sell, and those cheeses, as all of us knew, were not to be eaten.

One day, Mme. Durand sent me downstairs to bring up some potatoes. It was a very hot day, and the cellar was deliciously cool. It was deliciously fragrant as well. On the large table in the middle of the room lay a gigantic circle of Gruyère cheese. Even in the dim light it glowed like a yellow pearl. Its aroma was beguiling. I knew that there were cheeses upstairs that I could eat, and I knew that the beautiful yellow cheese that lay there on the table was intended for the market the following morning. I also knew that M. Durand took his cheeses very seriously, and that Mme. Durand could slap and shake as well as pinch.

But I could not stop myself. I rushed up to the cheese, took a bite out of one perfect side, and swallowed it all, almost in one gulp. It was delicious, but once it was down, I knew it had all been a big mistake.

The following morning we children were awakened by some loud cursing, and an even louder invitation on the part of M. Durand to accompany him downstairs. The light was now on, and the ravished cheese lay there on the table with one bite clearly torn out of its side. Nobody could mistake it for a hole.

"Who did it?" demanded M. Durand.

Everybody said not me.

"I want to know who did it," M. Durand thundered.

"And when I find out, I will break every bone in his body. I will crack open his head. I will beat him within an inch of his life. Now—who did it?"

Jacqueline and the two youngest boys began to cry.

"Gabriel!" shouted M. Durand to his oldest son, a boy of about my age, "did you do it?"

"No, Papa," Gabriel said.

"Jean-Pierre," bellowed M. Durand to his second boy, who was about six, "was it you?"

"No, Papa," wept Jean-Pierre.

"Célestin," shouted M. Durand, "you?"

Little Célestin was younger than Jacqueline. He was about three then, and was crying so hard he couldn't even answer. All he could do was shake his head—no.

M. Durand then looked at me. "Nicole, was it you?" he yelled.

"No, Monsieur."

"Well, then, Jacqueline, did you do it?"

Jacqueline was crying. Tears lay on her long, curling lashes, and her blue eyes were like round marbles. She shook her bright, red curls and sobbed, "No, Monsieur. Maybe it was Hitler."

Hitler was the name of the dog.

"It was not Hitler," M. Durand shouted. "He knows better than to take a bit out of my cheeses." He narrowed his eyes, and put his hands on his hips. "One of you is guilty, I know. Now who was it. I warn you, the longer you keep me waiting, the sorrier you will be."

Mme. Durand broke in. "Jacques," she said, "it was neither Jacqueline or Célestin. Jacqueline was in bed all day yesterday with a cold, and Tante Louise took Célestin away with her for the day."

"Ah!" M. Durand waved away the two youngest, and concentrated on the three eldest. He walked up and down, considering, and then finally he faced us, smiling. But it was not a pleasant smile.

"Stay here!" he ordered.

He approached the plundered cheese, and cut three pieces out of it.

"Here!" he said, returning to us. "I want your opinion of this cheese. You first, Nicole. Take a bite out of this piece—a big bite—right here."

I bit without thinking. I nearly choked on it. By this morning I had lost my taste for cheese.

"Gabriel, here!" Gabriel bit.

"Jean-Pierre!" The same.

"Aha!" M. Durand carried the three pieces over to the large cheese, and compared them with the original bite. "Madeleine," he said, addressing his wife, "come here!" She joined him, and looked. Without a word, they both turned and faced me.

"NICOLE!"

M. Durand did not break every bone in my body, nor did he crack open my head, but my rear end was sore that day, and Mme. Durand pinched my arm several times and said that if I stopped eating like a bird at mealtimes, and took more nourishment, I wouldn't have to go around committing crimes in between meals.

They were strict but they had taken care of us since we were babies, and treated us like their own children. Which wasn't good, but at least we never felt we were treated worse than their own children. Actually, M. Durand probably was nicer to me than to any of the others. Sometimes I even sat in his lap after supper, and he patted my shoulder and jiggled me on his knee.

I was used to them, and I was not unhappy. But every Friday night when our parents came to see us, starting from when I was six or seven, I would ask, "Why can't we live with you?"

"Because we can't afford it yet."

"Why can't you afford it? Georges Morel at school, lives with his mother. His father is dead and his mother is a laundress. They are very poor, but Georges and his two sisters, Louise and Eugénie, are at home."

"Soon. We are doing the best we can."

"But why do we have to wait? I can take care of the house while you and Papa work. I can boil eggs and make coffee."

"We have no room for you. You know that Papa and I live in that one tiny room in the boardinghouse."

"Jacqueline and I won't mind. We can sleep on the floor, and we don't eat much. Mme. Durand says we eat like birds."

"Now listen to me, Nicole. As soon as we can, we will. Papa and I are just as anxious as you to be together again."

"No, you are not. If you were, nothing would stop you. You just don't care for us."

"Now, Nicole, I don't like the way you are talking. Sometimes, I'm afraid you forget yourself."

Then one night, Maman told us that she had found an

apartment, and that the following week would be our last with the Durands. They would come for us the next Friday night and we would go "home." I thought about "home" all through that week, and imagined how it would look with new and bright furniture and pretty pictures hanging on the walls.

It was disappointing when we walked into the apartment on the Avenue du Petit Port. There were four small rooms, and a tiny, dark kitchen. None of the furniture was new, and there were no pictures hanging on the wall.

Jacqueline didn't mind. She bounced up and down on the large double bed that she and I would share and which took up most of our room.

"Come here, Nicole," Maman said. She opened the doors of the living room, and we were outside on a *veranda,* an enclosed sun-porch with windows on all sides that could be raised way up.

"Wait until the morning," Maman said. "You will be able to see Mont Revard."

Everything seemed so strange the next day. Papa had already left for work, but Maman was staying home to get everything in order. She sent me down to the *crèmerie* to buy some Brie cheese, and she gave me a milk pail which I was to have filled with milk.

I had never bought anything in a store before. Mme. Durand baked her own bread, and milk was delivered by a local farmer. Maman showed me from the *veranda* how I must walk up to the end of the street, turn the corner, and there in the middle of that street was the *crèmerie.*

I held the coins tightly in my hand and walked slowly up the street. This was my street. All the trees and the houses with their red-tiled roofs and the people who lived inside them belonged to me now. I felt happy and important. I had a street, and an apartment, and a mother and father who lived with me. My mother had sent me out with money in my hand to shop for her. It was all so beautiful—the bright, clear day, the fine street, the feel of the hard coins in my hand. And times like this were now forever.

In the *crèmerie,* two bright-eyed, skinny, little women stood behind the counter. They looked like twins, but they were only sisters. Mlle. Hélène and Mlle. Jeanette Frenay, owners of the store.

"Yes?" demanded Mlle. Hélène.

"Please, Madame," I said, "may I have a piece of Brie cheese."

"What is your name?" asked Mlle. Jeanette.

"Nicole Nieman."

"Where do you live?" continued Mlle. Hélène.

"Around the corner—on the Avenue du Petit Port."

"I have never seen you before," said Mlle. Hélène.

"No, Madame, we just moved in yesterday."

"Ah, and what rental do you pay?" asked Mlle. Jeanette.

"I don't know, Madame."

"Well, well . . . and what do you want?"

"A piece of Brie cheese."

"It's not very good today," remarked Mlle. Hélène.

I glanced at the large, round Brie cheese in one of the

cases. It had a triangular piece cut out of it and looked creamy and smooth inside.

"My mother told me to buy a piece of Brie," I insisted.

Mlle. Jeanette picked up a knife. "The Camembert is delicious today," she said.

"But Madame, my mother . . ."

She sliced a piece off the Camembert, wrapped it in white paper, and said, "Your mother will appreciate the Camembert. What else do you need?"

I handed her my milk pail, and she filled it with milk.

"My greetings to your mother," said Mlle. Jeanette, taking my money. "We will look forward to meeting her."

Maman thought the Camembert was delicious, and said she had heard from the landlady that the two sisters in the *crèmerie* were strange, but that their cheeses were excellent.

Jacqueline and I sat at the table in the kitchen while Maman fixed our *café-au-lait,* and cut us large slices of bread and cheese. She fussed over us, asking us if the coffee was too hot, or if we wanted more cheese, but she didn't insist that we eat anything. Jacqueline kept kicking her chair but Maman didn't even notice. She was laughing and talking to us about how much fun it was going to be, and how once we had some money, we would buy new furniture, and maybe even a rug for the living room. Maman's hair and eyes were very dark, and her face always seemed to be moving.

After breakfast, I helped Maman unpack the dishes and the pots and put them away in the pantry. Maman had part of a set of beautiful china dishes. They were white with a border of tiny, delicate roses around the rim. The cups were very fancy. There were only five of them with gold twisted handles and little gold legs.

"There is a china closet I have my eye on," Maman said. "If we continue to do as well as we have been doing, perhaps one day I can buy it and display some of our pretty things." She wiped the cups carefully, and began to put them away.

"Maman, may I hold one too?" I asked.

"Yes, Nicole, but be very careful. They are quite delicate."

I held the cup in my hands and ran my fingers all along the border of little roses, and underneath I touched the tiny gold feet.

"Oh, Maman, it's so beautiful!"

"Maman, I want to hold a cup too," said Jacqueline. Maman hesitated.

"Don't let her, Maman," I said. "She'll drop it. You can't trust her."

"Yes I can. I can." Jacqueline cried.

"Of course you can," Maman said. "Come here, near me, and you can hold it over these towels. Be careful now."

Jacqueline held the cup very carefully over the towels on the table. She was smiling. Then she looked over at me, and made a funny face.

"Maman, Jacqueline made a funny face at me."

Maman took the cup from Jacqueline. "Who wants to put away the sheets and pillowcases?" she asked.

"I do."

"I do."

It was a happy day—putting everything away, dusting the furniture, cleaning the floors of our apartment. It was a happy day, especially for me. But for Jacqueline, it was not all happy.

Around three in the afternoon, she stood with her back against the living room wall, and said, "I want Hitler."

"What?" said Maman. "You want what?"

"Hitler," Jacqueline said. She began whining and stamping her foot. "I want Hitler! I want Hitler!"

Maman looked at her, very puzzled.

I started to laugh. "She wants our dog—I mean the dog we had at the Durands. She always played with him a lot, and M. Durand said he liked her the best."

"I want Hitler," Jacqueline shouted.

"Now, *chérie,* you know you can't have a dog here. But we will go and visit the Durands very often, maybe even this Sunday."

"I want him *now!* I want him *now!*" She was stamping her feet and really shouting.

"Now," I told Maman, "it's time for her nap. Jacqueline, go and lie down and take a nap."

"No!"

"Well then, Maman will have to smack you or pinch you."

"Nicole!" said Maman.

"Oh, but that's the only way to handle her," I told Maman. "You don't know what she's like when she's tired. Mme. Durand always gave her a little pinch or smack when she didn't listen, and you'll see, once she has her nap she will be much nicer."

Maman was looking at Jacqueline helplessly. By now Jacqueline was jumping up and down and screaming.

"Just do what I tell you, Maman. I really know her better than you."

"Do you?" Maman said. She moved forward and reached out for Jacqueline, who put up her hands to protect herself. Maman picked Jacqueline up, kicking and struggling, and spoke softly to her. "Now, now, *ma poupée*, now, now."

She sat down, and held her in her lap, and Jacqueline sobbed and sobbed and sobbed.

"Maman," I insisted, "if you would only . . ."

"Be still, Nicole, you don't *always* know everything."

After a while Jacqueline stopped sobbing, and struggling. She put her finger in her mouth, and lay her head against Maman's shoulder, and fell asleep.

Maman smiled at me and whispered, "You see."

I felt foolish and went out onto the *veranda*. We had raised the windows because the day was warm. I leaned out, and looked at Mont Revard off in the distance, the train track up the street, and all the little houses with plane trees in front of them. I could hear the train approaching and concentrated on the sound of its wheels coming closer and closer, its whistle blasting in the air. Across the street, a man looked out of a window and smiled at me. I waved at him and he waved back. I could see some children coming up the street now on their way home from school.* Tomorrow was Sunday, and on Mon-

* French children go to school on Saturday, and stay home on Thursday.

day I would start school too. Maybe one of those children would be my friend. I watched them walking up the street. There was a boy walking by himself. Behind him came two boys together, and behind them, four or five girls. One of the girls—she was wearing a blue coat and a blue and white beret—ran into one of the houses across the street. She looked about my age, and she had dark hair like me. As she was just about to go through the door of her house, she turned and looked right up at me. I wanted to smile or wave, but I felt shy, and turned in the direction of the train tracks. Soon the train came jugging by, and when I turned back she was gone.

I watched as other children came up the street, and as some of them were absorbed into the houses. Then I thought about the girl in the blue and white beret. I leaned on the partition and I watched the street. Sure enough, there they came—two girls, walking together, arms around each other. One was the girl across the street in her blue and white beret, and the other—was me—wearing a new beret. It was blue and white too. I had to lean all the way out because they stopped downstairs in front of my house. They laughed, and pushed each other, and then they both came running into the house. I could hear their footsteps coming up the stairs, their laughter, the door to the apartment opening. I wheeled around to watch them come in.

There was only me, leaning against the window wall, and smiling at myself for being such a silly daydreamer. But perhaps on Monday . . . Now that I was with my parents, anything could happen.

26

I walked back into the apartment. Maman was still sitting in the chair holding Jacqueline, fast asleep, her thumb still in her mouth.

"Why don't you put her down on the bed, Maman? She might sleep an hour and a half or even two hours."

Maman shook her head, smiled at me, and then looked down, smiling at Jacqueline. Around her lay the boxes of belongings still to be put away. I shook my head, gathered up an armful of towels and walked toward the cupboard. *Somebody* had to see that things got done.

November 1938

I AM NOT," I said out loud, but nobody heard me.

". . . bossy, and lacking in respect toward grownups." My mother was excited, and she was speaking very quickly, slurring some of her words.

"I am not," I said, but this time I said it loud enough so they could hear.

"Be still!" Maman said. "You'll wake up Jacqueline."

I climbed out of bed, and padded into the living room where both of my parents were sitting, talking about me. My mother always spoke openly when she was angry. She never kept secrets, because she couldn't keep secrets. All day long her annoyance had been buzzing around me, and tonight as soon as Papa came home she had let it all out completely.

"You have no idea how embarrassed I was," said Maman. "Mme. Thibault was waiting for me to finish the hem on her skirt"—Maman now did sewing at home—"and began to talk very pleasantly with Nicole. When I was finished, she tried on the skirt, and Nicole said, 'Mme. Thibault, I don't think you should wear colors like red and white. You should wear dark blue because fat people look better in dark blue or black.' "

"And it's true," I said.

"Yes, but nobody asked you for your opinion," said Maman. "And if you keep on giving it, I will lose all my customers, and what will happen to us then?"

I shrugged my shoulders and put my face into the Who

Cares look. I put my hands on my hips, and stood there with my legs spread apart.

"Well," said Papa, "perhaps it only happened this one time. I'm sure that after this Nicole will try not to be so outspoken."

"Oh?" said Maman. "If it was only this one time, I wouldn't be so annoyed. But Nicole is very free with her mouth, and her opinions are numerous. She is continually telling me how to clean house, how to cook, how to take care of Jacqueline . . ."

"I've been with Jacqueline all these years so I know her best."

"Be still," Maman shouted. Her cheeks were very pink, and her eyes looked even darker than usual. She was angry. I looked down at my shoes and shut up.

"There is no subject on which she is not an authority. Even at school, Mlle. Legrand tells me there are problems. She does not read as well as the other children. As a matter of fact, she hardly read at all when she first started school. Mlle. Legrand says she cannot imagine what they taught her in the other school. And her handwriting—Mlle. Legrand says it is worse than all the other children, even the seven-year-olds, and Nicole is nearly nine. Mademoiselle says there are days when Nicole simply will not learn. Even when she raps her knuckles, Nicole will just look up at her with that face she's wearing now, refusing to learn. And sometimes, she even tells Mlle. Legrand—"

"I hate Mlle. Legrand. She's a *vieille vache.*"

Maman slapped me, and I started crying. "You see, you see," she said to Papa, and Papa was talking to both of us at the same time. "Don't be so fresh . . . best thing is not to lose your temper . . . where did you ever learn such an expression . . . she's very intelligent and independent. She can be reasoned with . . . stop crying like that . . ."

My father had a long face. His hair was red, but not bright and shiny like Jacqueline's. It was a quiet red, and his face was a quiet, mournful face. Maman's face always showed how she was feeling, but Papa's thoughts lay inside him, hidden.

I was weeping noisily but watching him carefully from under my wet eyelashes.

Maman was watching him too. He looked at me, and then he looked at her. I sniffed loudly, and I watched as she wrinkled up her forehead and waited for him to say something.

"I'm hungry," he said.

I stopped crying, and Maman repeated, "Hungry?"

"Yes, Henriette. Remember, I've just come back from Paris, and I didn't have time to eat anything there what with buying all the new stock, and getting it to the station in time to make the train."

"Oh, you poor man!" Maman said apologetically. "And as soon as you come in, I fill your ears with all sorts of silly little things. Ah—what's the matter with me! But wait, just a minute—I'll have some soup for you and cheese and fruit."

Maman hurried into the kitchen and Papa beckoned for me to come to him. He put an arm around me, shook his head and said, "I cannot imagine where you get such a big mouth from."

"I think from Maman," I said. "I think I'm a lot like her."

"I think so too," Papa said. "And that's a good thing. But Maman never says anything that hurts anyone."

"She hurts me."

"And Maman never had your chance—and neither did I—at a good education. Both of us hope you will grow up to be an accomplished, educated woman but in order to do that you have to listen now more than you talk."

"But, Papa, I have a lot to say."

"It's a problem, I admit," he said.

"Come in now, David," Maman soon called. "Everything is ready."

Papa stood up.

"Please, Papa, can I come and sit with you while you eat?"

"If you think you can sit there and not make your mother angry."

"I'll try, Papa."

Maman had the table set for Papa. She had a bowlful of soup, some bread, and a large piece of Camembert.

Papa began eating, and Maman said to me, "Are you hungry, Nicole? Would you like some cocoa?"

She was smiling. Maman never stayed angry once she had exploded. It was as if she had forgotten all about our argument.

"Yes, I am hungry," I said. "And may I have some bread and cheese, too?"

I resolved not to be so free with my opinions, even though they were usually right. In the days that followed I found myself choking down most of the suggestions I wanted to make to my mother and swallowing all of the others. And still my mother complained that I had a big mouth.

My friend Françoise did not think I had a big mouth. She agreed that my mother was being unreasonable. Françoise said that even though my mother was unreasonable, hers was even more so. Françoise was rich. Her father was a doctor and her mother stayed at home, and didn't have to do anything. There was a servant to take care of Françoise and her little sister, Monique, and another servant to clean the house and cook the meals. Françoise's mother, Mme. Rosten, was the most beautiful woman I ever saw. All of her was always in place—her hair, her blouse, her stockings, her shoes. Nothing ever wrinkled or looked worn. In the summertime she was always cool, and seemed untouched by the heat.

I had visited Françoise's house a number of times, and had occasionally eaten dinner or supper there. It was a great, big, rich house, and I never knew which spoon to use when we were eating, or how to answer the questions Dr. and Mme. Rosten asked me. They were very kind but I always felt clumsy and stupid. Mostly I giggled when I spoke to them.

Françoise loved coming to my house, and most of the time, when we were not out of doors, we spent on the *veranda*.

"There," I said, "Mme. Fiori is sweeping her steps again. Two times a day, Mme. Fiori sweeps her steps. Once in the morning, when Lucie and Antoine leave for school, and once in the afternoon, when they return."

"Let's play *Aux Dames,*" said Françoise, not even looking.

"Sometimes Lucie has to sweep, but she never does. I mean, she just pushes the broom down the steps, and watches the window in case her mother is looking out. But she never really sweeps anything up."

Françoise was setting up the board. "I want black," she said. "Will you take white?"

I was interested in everything that concerned Lucie and her family. Lucie was the girl in the blue and white beret whom I hoped would be my first friend. But she did not become my first friend. She hated me and I never knew why. To me, everything about her was fascinating—the way her dark hair curled toward her face on the right side, and away from it on the left, how she walked with strong, hard steps, her skirt slapping against her legs, and the strange way she had of laughing, with her lips parted but her teeth clenched.

She was admired by the other girls, but not as much as Marie or Françoise. And here was I, a newcomer to the school, lucky enough to be singled out by one of the most admired girls in my class for a friend. I knew I was lucky. I was happy and comfortable with Françoise, and always looked forward to our times together.

But I longed for Lucie's friendship. I ached for it. Perhaps because she was the first girl I had noticed when we first came to stay with our parents, she seemed to mean something very special to me. When Lucie spoke to me (and she never did unless she had to), or passed me some paper in school, I was happier than if someone else had paid me a compliment.

36

I tried to please her. I laughed at her jokes, agreed with her opinions, and copied the way she walked. But she seemed to loathe me. She went out of her way to insult me and to point out to others how stupid I was, how clumsy, how old my clothes were. Some days when I tried particularly hard to win her favors, if I offered her a sweet, or admired something she was wearing, and she could not find any reason to be nasty, she would just turn away, but I could feel the anger inside her.

And I never knew why.

Lucie did not interest Françoise at all. We seldom spoke of her. It would have been impossible, in any case, for me to tell another person how much I admired Lucie and how interested I was in anything that concerned her.

I watched Lucie's house every opportunity I had, and I had many from my *veranda*. I knew all about the outside of the house, and as much as I could about the inside. I knew the color of the curtains at each window, and I also knew that there was a piano in front of the living room window downstairs. I knew that Lucie's grandmother sat in a rocking chair at one of the upstairs windows and seemed to watch everything that happened on the street. Often she seemed to be looking at me, and in the beginning I would smile at her or wave, but she never responded. I thought perhaps it might be a family trait to dislike me, but I learned later that the old woman had cataracts and did not see very well.

I watched as Marie or Georgette or Suzanne entered the house after school. Once there was a party that even

Françoise attended, and many others in my class—but not me, never me. Sometimes I would lean my head against the glass windows of the *veranda,* and concentrate hard on the living room curtains. And then it would happen. I would go beyond them, into a lovely room with bright, new furniture and a shining piano. Lucie would be seated at the piano, playing, and she would smile at me and move over on the piano bench so that I could sit down next to her and watch her quick, slim fingers pressing the keys. And she would play any song I liked.

The *veranda* was the best part of the house. There were four chairs and an old table with a white porcelain top that had numerous black chips (I counted them—there were twelve large chips and twenty-three small ones). That was all the furniture, but Françoise and I could play *Aux Dames* or cards around it. Maman could do her hand sewing, and the whole family used the table as a desk. Every Sunday, except for the very hottest or the very coldest days, we ate our dinner on the *veranda.*

The *veranda* was where I went when I wanted to be by myself. I would gather up some pillows and perhaps an old blanket, and tuck myself into one corner of the back wall. From down there, I could see the sky, and I could read or think or cry and be alone.

Even if Maman was in the room, sewing or talking to Jacqueline, the corner still belonged to me, especially if I had a book in my hands. As long as Maman saw me reading, she seldom disturbed me. Sometimes Jacqueline insisted on sharing the corner with me, but most of the time she would be busy playing with her doll, and begging Maman for scraps of material.

"See, Maman, Danielle needs a pink hat with a little piece of veil, and then she will be all dressed and ready to go to church."

"Well then, she shall have a little piece of this pink satin, and if you go and look in the small blue box in my bedroom, there are some scraps of black and white and maybe blue veiling."

"I know, Maman. I just looked, and may I have a piece of the white veiling?"

"Yes."

"May I have all of the white veiling?"

"You just said you wanted only a piece."

"Yes, but Danielle wants a shawl to go with her hat, and then she will be the fanciest lady in the whole world."

"Then I think she had better have it."

"Maman."

"Yes?"

"Why don't we go to church any more, the way we used to when we lived with the Durands?"

"Because the Durands are Catholic, and believe it is important to go to church every Sunday."

"Aren't all of us Catholic?"

"No, *ma poupée,* we are Jewish."

"And don't we have to go to church too?"

"Many Jewish people go to church, only they call it synagogue. But your Papa and I don't believe that we have to go to synagogue."

"I'm glad, because I hated going to church. It was boring, and Mme. Durand always pinched my legs just because I moved a tiny little bit."

"I think perhaps you may have moved more than just a tiny little bit. But now that you're home with Papa and me you can wiggle as much as you like. That is, until you start school. Then you must sit still, and listen to your teacher."

"Will she pinch me if I don't?"

"I don't think she will."

"Nicole, does your teacher pinch you?"

"No, but she raps my fingers with her ruler, and she makes me stand in front of the class if I don't do the work exactly as she says. I hate her. I hope you have Mlle. Martelle or Mme. Chardin. Anybody but Mlle. Legrand."

"Nicole," Maman says, looking at her sewing, and snipping off a piece of thread, "Mlle. Legrand may be strict but it is for your own good. You say you want to be a doctor when you grow up, and Papa and I think that would be wonderful, but in order to be a doctor you must be very disciplined. You must read and write and understand mathematics. You must not fight your teachers, but accept their lessons gratefully . . ."

"Mlle. Legrand is a *vieille*—"

Maman sat motionless for a moment, frozen, waiting for me to finish. But I did not.

After a moment she said, "Mlle Legrand is possibly not the most understanding person in the world or the kindest, but she is a very highly educated person who really cares about her students' progress. We are lucky to have her in the school."

"I don't want to go to school, Maman," said Jacqueline, "and when I get to be six, and it is time for me to go to school, I'll run away with Danielle and nobody will ever find us."

"You won't get very far," I said. "The *gendarmes* will come looking for you, and they will find you, and put you in prison if you won't go. They will put you in the dungeon, and—"

"MAMAN!"

"What is that you are reading, Nicole?"

"Le Comte de Monte Cristo, Maman."

"I thought so. Why don't you go on reading, *chérie,* and be quiet."

"Yes, Maman."

"But Maman, Maman, will they come and put me in jail, in a dungeon?"

"No, *ma poupée.*" Maman laughed. "All that is in Nicole's book, but I really don't even think she is able to read it yet. She is just looking at the pictures now, but one day, after *she* has been in school a while longer, she will be able to read it. And you too, Jacqueline, after you go to school, you will be able to read many wonderful, exciting books. Just like Nicole."

"But I never will read *that* book Nicole is reading. I will only read happy books."

Maman gave Jacqueline a piece of pink satin, and Jacqueline wrapped it around her doll's head, and hummed as she played. Maman's scissors snipped, and sometimes her chair squeaked as she changed her position. I looked at another picture in *Le Comte de Monte Cristo*. They were throwing a sack with a man in it off a wall into the water. I closed the book, and lay back on a pillow, and watched the sky darken. Soon, it would be too dark to read or sew or see a pink hat on a doll, and soon Papa would be home.

December 1939

Mlle.
Legrand

"YOU MUST HAVE DONE SOMETHING for her to say such a thing to you," Papa said. "Try to remember."

And I did. But I had done nothing.

We had been singing the carols that morning, and Mme. Claude, the music teacher, kept nodding at us, and pointing upwards. And all the high voices had gone up, higher and higher, while those of us, like myself, who sang the alto parts tried to sing with deep, round sounds.

> "Il est né, le divin enfant
> Jouez hautbois, resonnez musettes
> Il est né, le divin enfant
> Chantons tous son avènement."

"Today," said Mme. Claude, "you are quite good. Except for a little weakness in the alto section, I cannot complain."

Which meant we had been outstanding. I turned to smile at Lucie, who had been placed next to me, and she said, "Dirty Jew!"

"What did you say?" I asked, still smiling, not understanding.

"I said you are a Dirty Jew," she said in a whisper, but quite clearly.

I nodded, meaning that I had heard her. But as she continued to look at me, waiting for me to respond, I tried to think of something to say. But all I could do was giggle.

45

It was not the right thing to do, because there was a bad feeling that stayed in my stomach the rest of the day. There was something that I should have said in reply instead of giggling, but I didn't know what.

I told my mother that afternoon. "Lucie Fiori called me a Dirty Jew."

"And what did you say?" she asked, her face angry almost immediately.

"I didn't say anything. I laughed."

"Laughed!"

"But Maman . . ." I knew she was angry at me—disappointed, too. "I didn't know what she meant so I didn't know what to say. What *is* a Dirty Jew? She is certainly mistaken about me because I am not a Dirty Jew. But I don't know who is."

"Nobody is. Nobody is," Maman said. "Never mind. It doesn't mean a thing. Just forget about it."

But as soon as Papa came home that night, she let it all out for him, and that was when he asked me what I had done or said to Lucie to make her call me a Dirty Jew.

"Nothing, Papa. She doesn't like me, I know. And she always insults me, even though I would like to be friends with her, and always try to be nice."

"Don't try any more," my mother said. "I want you to keep away from that girl. I want you to ignore her, and not to speak to her, and never to invite her here."

Which was funny, because even if I did invite her, she wouldn't come.

"But, Papa, what is a Dirty Jew? Is it a Jewish person who isn't clean?"

"No, Nicole. I'm afraid in the eyes of some people it is you and Maman and me and even Jacqueline."

"But I am not dirty, Papa."

"I know that, but there are people who hate the Jews, and make up all sorts of lies about them which are not true."

"Well, I had better tell Lucie that she is mistaken, and that she should not listen to lies."

"I don't think it would do any good, but you can try. It's always worth trying to make things better than they are."

"She doesn't have to try anything," Maman said. "I will handle the whole situation." She was busy, moving around the room, picking up the newspaper and putting it down, straightening the doilies on the furniture, plumping up the pillows.

"What will you do?" Papa asked.

"I will go to school tomorrow, and speak to Mlle. Legrand."

I sat on my father's lap, and asked, "Is Mlle. Legrand a Jew?"

"No, Nicole. In this town there are very few Jewish families. Besides ourselves, there are the Rostens—Françoise's family, the Simons, the Morels—a few others. Nearly all of our friends are not Jewish. The Henris are not, the Latours, the Bernards . . ."

"I don't think I want to be Jewish," I said, and Maman said, "Shame on you. Just because some ignorant little fool insults you, you are ready to run away and be like everybody else."

"I want to be like everybody else," I said.

"Yes," said my father, "and so do we all. But I'm afraid you can't stop being Jewish as long as other people think you are Jewish."

"I don't understand you."

"Now look here. Your mother and I came from very religious families. When we were your age we went to the synagogue, and prayed, and followed all the religious customs. I even thought I would be a rabbi. But when I grew up a little, I no longer wanted to be a rabbi, and I no longer wanted to go to the synagogue. But that doesn't mean because I no longer practice the religion that I stop being a Jew. I can't stop, even if I wanted to, because as long as people hate Jews, they will always see me as a Jew whether I call myself one or not."

"But nobody ever called me a Jew before."

"And nobody will again," Maman said, her mouth very tight, "when I am finished saying my piece tomorrow. This is not Germany where people allow that kind of thing. Thank Goodness we live in a country where a Jew is as good as anyone else."

"Maman," I asked, "do you think the reason Lucie Fiori hates me so much is because I am Jewish?"

"I am sure of it," Maman said.

"But she likes Françoise, and Françoise is Jewish. She admires Françoise, and I heard her bragging to Huguette about how splendid Françoise's house is, and how she had been there many times. But Françoise says the truth is that she has been there only once."

"Well, well," Maman said impatiently, "even bigots make exceptions. But I am certain, if she has always been so

48

nasty to you, that it must be because you are Jewish. What other reason could there be?"

I found my mother's opinion encouraging. If the only reason for Lucie's dislike was my Jewishness, well then there was hope. I could always say to Lucie, "I won't be Jewish any more if you will be my friend." But after thinking about it for a few minutes, I said, "No, Maman, she doesn't hate me only because I'm Jewish. She just hates me for everything I am. Even if I wasn't Jewish, she would hate me for everything else I was."

"That, of course, is possible too," said my father. "There was my brother, Reuben, a handsome, brilliant boy. All the girls liked him. They would giggle when he met them in the street, and turn their heads after he had passed. He was the most admired young man in the village—except for one girl. She couldn't stand him. And— who knows why—he fell in love with her. There was nothing special about her. She wasn't pretty, or charming, or even good-tempered. Her parents wanted her to marry my brother. Everybody was astonished, but she said no, and kept on saying no. She even ran away from home rather than put up with her parents' urging. Sometimes I think human beings will treasure something they cannot have and, in reverse, will despise a treasure that comes too easily."

"What foolishness!" Maman said. "What kind of story is that to be telling Nicole? There is no comparison at all. Believe me, she hates you because you are Jewish. Now go to bed, and don't worry. I will take care of the whole matter."

Maman arrived in school the following morning while we

were studying mathematics. She was dressed very fashion-ably. She wore her black hat, her black coat with the beaver collar, a white scarf, black leather gloves, and black pumps. She did not open her coat all the time she was there.

My mother's voice, it seemed to me, could be heard in every corner of the quiet classroom. The children listened to her complaint about Lucie. Their eyes traveled from Lucie to me and back to the two grownups at the front of the room.

It was hard to hear what Mlle. Legrand was saying. For the most part, she listened. My mother spoke faster and faster, and then finally she stopped and the room was quiet.

"Nicole, come up here, please. And you, Lucie, I want you here too. The rest of the class will continue on with the division problems. If I see anyone's head up, she will write a homework paper for me on Disobedience."

Maman looked so nice, I thought. You could see that her face had been made up with special care this morning —powder, rouge, lipstick, a little mascara, and around her, the fragrance of perfume. I felt proud of my mother.

In contrast, Mlle. Legrand wore just a thin line of lip-stick that cut across the true shape of her lips. She was a tall, square woman, and had to bend slightly to hear my mother.

"Lucie," said Mlle. Legrand, "Mme. Nieman has com-plained that you called Nicole a Dirty Jew yesterday. Is this true?"

Lucie did not reply.

"Is it true, Nicole?" Mademoiselle said, looking at me, but reaching out a hand for Lucie.

"Yes, Mademoiselle."

"Is it true, Lucie?" Mlle. Legrand put a hand on Lucie's arm, and moved her toward herself.

"Yes, Mademoiselle, it is true."

"I see, and may I ask why you called her that?"

Lucie shrugged her shoulders.

"Answer me, please."

"I don't know why."

"Do you, Nicole?"

"No, Mademoiselle."

"Had you teased Lucie, or insulted her in any way?"

"No, Mademoiselle."

"Had she, Lucie?"

"No, but she . . ."

"Yes?"

"No, Mademoiselle."

"Then I think you had better apologize to Nicole, and to Mme. Nieman, and perhaps to the class too for disturbing their lesson."

Lucie remained silent. I looked quickly at her face, and saw that she had her eyes down. Her face was very red, and she held her mouth shut tight.

I felt sorry for Lucie, and I didn't care if she apologized or not. I just hoped that she would stop hating me. Still, I was happy that my mother had come to school, looking so slim and fashionable, and smelling so nice.

Lucie remained silent.

"Lucie," Mlle. Legrand asked softly, "where were your parents born?"

"In Italy, Mademoiselle."

"Yes," said Mlle. Legrand, "and where were you born, Lucie?"

"In Italy, Mademoiselle, but I was an infant when we moved here."

"That may be so," said Mlle. Legrand, "but Nicole was born here." She spoke very gently. "I remind you of this, Lucie, because I believe you have behaved in a manner that is not French. As I think I have tried to teach you, France is a country that takes great pride in a very ancient and superior civilization. It is a country that has been generous with immigrants, and willing to offer a new home to people from foreign lands as long as they behave themselves. Nicole was born here. She is French even though she is Jewish. Now I think you had better apologize."

Lucie apologized. She was crying, but she apologized to me, to my mother, and to the class.

My mother did not look happy, but she thanked Mlle. Legrand, and they spoke a few minutes more about my work, and how I was improving. I could hear her accent, and knew she did not speak the same as most French people. My parents were born in Poland. Both had strong foreign accents, but I had never thought about it before.

Later, when I arrived home, Maman said she was happy that Lucie apologized, but she was not happy with the way Mlle. Legrand had handled the whole thing. What need was there, Maman said, to drag in the completely irrelevant matter about Lucie and her family being born in Italy? What difference did it make where they were born? Lucie had said something wrong and cruel, and needed to understand that she had, and to apologize. But nobody could help where he or she was born, and nobody ever had to apologize about that.

She spoke of it several times, but in the next few days another problem arose that took her mind off Lucie. It was Christmas. In previous years, our family had always been invited to one friend or another for Christmas dinner. This year, Maman had decided to prepare Christmas dinner, and she had invited nine guests—which meant thirteen people all together, counting our family. She could just fit ten around our dining room table, and three or four around the table on the *veranda,* which would have to be brought inside.

"We will just have to squeeze a little tighter," Papa said, "and Nicole and Jacqueline must make sure not to eat too much or there won't be any room at all."

Maman did not have enough dishes that matched. She had seven dinner plates in the fancy china set, and eight in the ordinary set. It was enough, but the dishes would all be different, which was too bad.

I told Françoise about the dishes, and she said, "But we have lots of extra dishes. I'll ask my mother."

The following afternoon, Françoise said, "Mme. Nieman, my mother says she would be very pleased if you borrowed a set of dishes from her. She has a service for twenty-four that she hardly ever uses."

"But where did you ever get the idea that I wanted to borrow dishes," Maman said, looking at me angrily.

"Nicole said you needed dishes, and we really have more—"

"Well, Nicole is mistaken. Please thank your mother very much from me, but we will have quite enough dishes. And then, I suppose, she will need extra dishes for Christmas herself."

"No, she won't. Usually we spend Christmas with my Uncle Georges and his family in Paris, and we have a wonderful time. But this year, Uncle Georges is in the hospital, and all our other relatives are either busy or traveling or going somewhere else. We will be staying home, and having Christmas dinner all by ourselves. I wish . . ." Françoise never finished what she was going to say.

I looked hard at my mother, but my mother avoided my eyes.

"It's not much fun," Françoise continued, "to be alone at Christmas."

My mother said quickly, "I'm sure we would be very happy, Françoise, if you and your family wanted to join us, but—"

"Oh, Mme. Nieman, how nice! How pleased Maman will be! I'm sure we can come. Nobody else invited us."

Maman said, "I had better send a note home with you. But, of course, if your mother has made other plans, we will understand."

Papa said that evening, "Where will you put everybody?"

"I don't know," said Maman. "And I don't know what they are all going to eat off. It's all because of Nicole. As I always tell you, she has a big mouth."

The Rostens accepted, and Mme. Rosten insisted that Maman borrow the dishes. She even had her cook's husband bring them over a few days before Christmas. Maman was nervous. Even though she now had enough dishes, and had borrowed a folding table and some chairs, she was nervous. It was all my fault, she kept on saying. People like the Rostens were used to the very finest of everything. They were rich. They were elegant. They were educated. How would they fit in? What could you talk to them about? Even Papa seemed nervous. Normally he drank very little wine and never smoked. But now he wondered if he should buy cigars for the men. Brandy? Special wines?

Maman was cooking a goose, stuffed with apples. The day before, she had baked apple tarts and a nut torte. The whole day the kitchen was filled with delicious smells. I was sent out on errands all through the day—to buy the cheese, the fruit, the bread.

All the tables and chairs were arranged in the dining room, and there was hardly any room to move about. Maman said she didn't know how she would serve, and everybody would be jammed in so tightly they would be uncomfortable. She knew it would be a disaster. And the goose seemed tough, and the fruit in the tarts was runny, and it was all my fault.

The guests started to arrive. The Rostens came first. They brought wine and brandy and chocolates and presents for Jacqueline and me. The presents were to go under the tree, and not be opened until tomorrow.

"It's a doll for Jacqueline, and a bracelet for you," Françoise whispered.

At first everybody seemed to get in everybody else's way. The Rostens kept saying how much they appreciated being invited, and my parents said it was a great pleasure for them. When the Henris and Latours arrived, the Rostens told each of them how kind it was of my parents to ask them, and my parents said it really was such a great pleasure. Nobody seemed to have much else to say except how cold it was, and did anyone think it would snow.

But after we sat down to eat, Jacqueline said there were so many legs under the table, she wasn't sure which was hers. Then everybody began to laugh, and it was so much fun even if we all were squashed together. The food was delicious—the goose wasn't tough and the tarts were very good even if the fruit was runny. Dr. Rosten told some stories about funny things that happened to him when he was in medical school. And the grownups kept laughing and laughing.

Papa offered cigars around, but Dr. Rosten said he never smoked. And then Maman started laughing and couldn't stop. Nobody knew why except Papa and me.

Later, the children went out on the *veranda*. Maman gave us a little tray of chocolates, nuts, and hard candies, and we sat outside, and munched, and whispered about what kind of presents we thought we were getting the next day. But it was too cold to stay out for very long. The other children went back inside first. Françoise and I stayed out a while longer. She said her parents had been nervous about coming. They didn't know what kind of people my parents were, but it seemed as if everybody was getting along very well. She said she was having a better time than she had ever had before on Christmas Eve, and she hoped the two of us could always spend it together.

I said I hoped so too. Then the two of us stood up to go inside. I could see through the windows of the *veranda* that all the lights were on in Lucie's house. And I wondered if she ever looked out one of her windows, and thought about what was happening in my house.

July 1940

THE WAR didn't really start for me until January 1940, when my father enlisted in the army.

"Why?" Maman kept demanding. "Why you? Why a man, thirty-eight years old, who has never handled a gun, and who has a wife and two young children? Why? . . . Why should such a man, and with a nervous stomach, too . . . why?"

Papa never answered all Maman's whys. He just kept saying the war would be over in no time, and probably he would be home in a few months.

He looked like somebody else in his uniform. Our Papa, who usually wore a cap, an old gray and blue sweater, and baggy pants. Our Papa, transformed into such a glamorous figure in his khaki uniform with the double row of gleaming gold buttons down the front of his long greatcoat, and a soldier's hat on his head.

We received letters from him at first and photographs, showing him with his companions. Papa was in the 71st Infantry Division, stationed a few miles outside of Sedan, near the Belgian border.

He wrote that he missed us all very much, and Maman was not to worry. He was warm and dry, and had plenty to eat. But it was too quiet, Papa said. It was boring. Everybody knew the Germans were afraid and were looking for a way out. Hitler could intimidate weak, little countries like Poland, Czechoslovakia, and Austria, but the combined strength of France and England must be giving him many a sleepless night. Since September, when Hitler invaded Poland, and England and France declared war on him, there hadn't been a peep out of Germany. Everybody knew that Germany was finished.

To me, the war meant that Papa was away. Nothing else was different.

But in May, Germany attacked Belgium, Holland, and Luxembourg. In a few days, the German army had invaded France. The newspapers and the radio spoke of our victories, but Holland surrendered and so did Belgium and Luxembourg.

When the German army attacked along the River Meuse, at the town of Sedan where Papa was stationed, Maman stayed home and listened to the radio for the four days that the battle lasted. Still the commentators on the radio spoke of victory, but at the end Sedan fell, and the Germans had won.

There were no more letters from Papa after that. In June, German soldiers marched up the Champs Élysées in Paris, and a few weeks later the armistice was signed. France had been defeated. Two thirds of France—in the north and the west—would be occupied by German troops. What was left—and that included our town of Aix-les-Bains—would be unoccupied. But now we had a different government, and Maréchal Pétain was our new Chief of State.

There was no news about Papa. Each day, after the mail arrived, Maman smiled. She wanted a letter from

Papa very much, but even more, she did not want a letter saying he had been killed, or had been taken as a prisoner of war.

It was nearly two months since we had heard from Papa. Maman wrote letters and went to see officials in the town. Nobody could tell her anything. All was in confusion. As French soldiers came through Aix-les-Bains back from the war, Maman tried to talk to them and find out if anybody had seen Papa or heard anything about his division. Nobody had seen Papa but one soldier said that the 71st Division had not fought—just ran.

But that had been nearly a month ago, and still Papa did not come. Sometimes, as the weeks went by, Maman did not seem to hear what people said. She was listening for other sounds. One night, I heard her get out of bed and open the outside door. She whispered, "David?" and I came running out of bed, thinking Papa had returned. But no one was there.

Ever since the early part of June, refugees from Paris and other parts of occupied France had been streaming through Aix-les-Bains. Some were headed for Switzerland while others were looking for any place to stay where they could be safe from the Germans.

Our town always had many people coming in the summertime—sick people who came to take the thermal baths and drink the waters, and well people who came for fun—to enjoy the beautiful beaches along the Lac du Bourget, and all the special summer entertainments. There were concerts in the park, gambling in the casino, and plays in the theater. In the summer the population of Aix-les-Bains was two or three times what it normally was.

And now, this summer, there were many more people than usual. But they had not come for the waters or the summer amusements. For weeks now, the town was bursting with them. At the *crèmerie,* you had to wait on a line that sometimes stretched out into the street, and often you were lucky to get any cheese at all. M. Lantin, the baker, had hired two extra men and was now baking days as well as nights, but the bread tasted different. It was not as good.

Every night at our house, there were at least one or two guests for dinner, and sometimes they stayed the night. They told stories—frightening, sickening stories. Maman would glance at Jacqueline or me, and once she even shook her head, and nobody spoke until we left the room. Most of the guests were Jewish.

I didn't believe those stories. I asked Jacqueline if she believed them. Sometimes at night we heard the grown-ups talking and even crying while we lay in bed. Jacqueline said she believed the stories. She said maybe the Germans would come and take away Danielle, her doll, and put her in prison. Sometimes she cried, and then I held her and told her stories about Atlantis, and she felt better. Sometimes she didn't. Sometimes Maman had to come in and take Jacqueline into her own bed.

Berthe and Isaac came to us toward the end of June. They were cousins of Maman, and had run away from Hitler first from a village called Turek in Poland and then from Paris. Berthe was very fat. She put curlers in her hair every night, and sang songs all day. Isaac liked to kiss her. Maman said they were newlyweds, but when I asked her, Berthe said they had been married nearly two years.

"How can you call them newlyweds?" I asked Maman. "They have been married nearly two years."

"Yes," said Maman, "but they really haven't had a chance to enjoy being married. They've had to keep on running away from the Germans, first from Poland and now from Paris."

"But now they won't have to run any more, will they, Maman? The Germans will never come here, will they?"

"I hope not," Maman said. "They have signed a treaty, saying they will stay in the occupied part of France, but they have signed other treaties which they have broken."

Berthe and Isaac decided to remain in Aix-les-Bains. Isaac was a carpenter, and he went around looking for a job, but nobody needed him. There weren't enough jobs to go around. Maman said he could help her with the business until Papa came home. She also said they could stay with us until they found a place for themselves. Jacqueline and I slept in Maman's bed, and Isaac and Berthe slept in our bed. When Papa came home, I could sleep on the sofa and Jacqueline could sleep in two chairs pushed together.

Now Maman and Isaac left early in the morning for the markets. When we came home from school, we found Berthe waiting for us with our favorite snack of bread and butter and chocolate, and hot tea. Berthe only went out of the house to do the shopping. The rest of the time she stayed indoors, and cooked and cleaned, and curled her hair and polished her fingernails. She was always polishing her fingernails, and she did ours too. Sometimes she did our toenails. She had many little bottles of fingernail polish, and let us choose the color we wanted. Once Jacqueline asked her to use a different color on each fingernail, and she did.

She was so fat that her fingers looked like little pink sausages. But her skin was beautiful, and when she put rouge on her cheeks, they were like soft, juicy peaches. In the afternoon, if we stayed in, Berthe sang songs for us—all about love and fickle girls and unfaithful men. Most of the songs were in Yiddish or Polish.

She told us how Isaac lived in the same town as she but never noticed her, although she had always noticed him. One day, when she was all dressed up, very beautifully, in a dark purple dress, and wearing the same shade of fingernail polish that Jacqueline was presently wearing, she sat near him at a café, and they began talking. One thing led to another, and here they were, happily married.

Berthe believed in dressing up for a man. On most days she tried to put on a clean dress, comb her hair out, and have her fingernails all done by the time he came home. But sometimes she forgot to take out the curlers, or other times if she took out the curlers, she might forget to put on a clean dress. But Isaac never seemed to notice. You could hear his quick footsteps hurrying up the stairs. He would burst into the room, and not stop until he found her.

It was very romantic but it was a pity that she was fat, and that he had such large, yellow teeth.

Sometimes Berthe sat outside on the *veranda* with us. Now that it was July, we kept the windows open most of the time. I could lean out and watch for Papa.

Jacqueline and Berthe were sitting around the table looking through some magazines, and talking about clothes.

"You see this white voile dress with the sweetheart neckline, and the lace on the hem? Well, I had a dress exactly like that, with a little fuller sleeve, and a strawberry pattern instead of the rose—but otherwise just the same—and that was when Isaac took me to the movies for the first time. I wore it with a pink flower in my hair, and a pair of shoes—I still have them—white, with very high heels. I'll show them to you. But *oiy,* they were so tight, I could hardly walk. But the dress, I had to leave in Poland. We left so fast, I had to leave most of my nice things."

"Here, look at this one, Berthe. Isn't it pretty?"

"I don't know. It's not my color, and it's very matronly."

"What's my color, Berthe?"

"Your color? With a face like yours, every color is your color. Of course, some people say that pink is not a good color for redheads."

"But I love pink."

"Now I don't say it, but some people say it."

"Maman said she'll make me a pink dress for the summer, and a matching one for Danielle."

"Your Maman, she certainly is a wonder! But I had a friend who had red hair. She wasn't a beauty like you, but still she managed to get a husband, and she used to wear green all the time."

"I hate green."

The breeze was warm, and it was good feeling my hair blowing against my cheek. For days now, I had been watching for my father, and today, I was going to try a charm that my classmate, Marie, told me about. You had to close your eyes, cross them, and say the name of the person you wanted to work the spell on backwards. Then you uncrossed your eyes, opened them, and holding your breath you said what you wanted to happen. I knew how to say my father's name backwards—NAMEIN DIVAD.

I looked up the street and saw Jacques Romaines and Jean Flandin on their bikes, Mme. Henri and her daughter carrying packages and hurrying along the street.

I closed my eyes, but it did not seem to me that I was able to cross them when they were closed. So I opened them again, crossed them, closed them, but I felt they became uncrossed once I closed them. I wondered if the spell would work if I kept my eyes open. I opened my eyes, and there, coming up the street, was my father.

"Papa," I screamed, "Papa, Papa, Papa!"

He had been moving slowly up the street, but when I began calling he started to run. I yelled to Jacqueline and Berthe, "It's Papa. Really—it's Papa!" Then I rushed through the apartment, down the stairs, and up into his arms, just as he was about to open the downstairs door.

"Papa!"

He had been sick. First his toe had been broken by a car, driven by officers in his division who were fleeing from the battle at Sedan. Still he had managed to keep in front of the Germans, but later there had been fever and cramps, perhaps from some water he drank. For weeks he lay in a makeshift hospital. The doctor had promised to notify us. He thought we knew where he was.

Maman made him get into bed after she came home. All of us sat around him in the bedroom, and he told us how there had been no fighting, just running, how they had been betrayed by their leaders.

"But you're home, David," my mother said, "and you're safe."

My father shook his head. "They've taken France, and soon it will be England. Nobody is safe."

"Don't worry about it now," Maman said softly. She plumped up the pillows, and smoothed the blankets. "Rest now. Sleep! It will all work out, you'll see." She took Jacqueline by the hand, and the rest of us stood up.

"But Papa," Jacqueline said, "where is my present?"

"Present?"

"You promised, Papa." Jacqueline was close to tears. "You said when you came home you would bring me a present."

Maman shook her head, and said, "What a time to ask for presents. Thank God, Papa is home safe. What is the matter with you?"

Big tears rolled down Jacqueline's cheeks. She bit her lip but didn't say anything.

"Of course," Papa said. "How could I forget? Go,

chérie, look in my knapsack. Down toward the bottom. There is something for you, and something for Nicole. All those months we sat around waiting and waiting. I didn't forget. And look for something wrapped in a scarf, too. That's for Maman."

There were two lockets that he had made out of wood. They were heart-shaped, and one had a fancy J on it, and the other had an N. The locket was hinged, and opened up for pictures.

Papa had made a box for Maman. It was inlaid with many different pieces of wood, and was very beautiful.

"But David," Maman said, "I can't believe it. You never did anything like this before. You hardly knew how to hammer in a nail."

"There was nothing else to do," Papa said. "Thousands and thousands of soldiers, sitting and waiting with nothing to do."

"Maman." Jacqueline had hung her locket on a pink ribbon, and kept looking down at it on her chest. "Please, Maman, may I look through the pictures? I want you on one side and Papa on the other. Please, Maman, may I look at the pictures now—*right now!*"

Papa slid down under the covers, and closed his eyes. "But it's good to be home," he said.

October 1941

FOR THREE NIGHTS nobody had slept over at our house. Sunday morning, Jacqueline went bouncing around singing at the top of her lungs.

> *"Malbrouck s'en va-t-en guerre*
> *Mironton, Mironton, Mirontaine*
> *Malbrouck s'en va-t-en guerre*
> *Ne sait quand reviendra*
> *Ne sait quand reviendra*
> *Ne sait quand reviendra."*

She climbed on the sofa and the chairs in the living room, and crept under the dining room table.

"Jacqueline," I said, "stop it. You'll wake Maman and Papa."

But she didn't stop, and I was enjoying myself too. It was good not having anybody sleeping on the sofa. It was better not having to creep silently around the house, and have Maman say, Shh, you'll wake this one or that one. I knew Maman and Papa were awake anyway. They were so used to getting up around five every day that even on Sundays they seldom slept past six or six-thirty.

They were awake, in bed, talking to each other, and they smiled when Jacqueline came bounding in, and leaped into the bed, snuggling right between them.

"No more people," she announced. "I don't want any more people coming here ever, ever, ever, ever, ever, ever, ever . . ."

"That's enough, Jacqueline," Maman said.

". . . ever, ever, ever, ever . . ."

"That's ENOUGH!"

"Ever!"

I jumped into bed with them too, and my mother put an arm around me. She was wearing a peach-colored rayon nightgown, and I laid my head on her shoulder and felt the coldness of her nightgown on part of my face, and the warmth of her skin on the other part.

"Why do they always have to come here?" I said. "Why do we always have to be the ones who get stuck? The Rostens never have people staying over, and they have much more room than we do."

Maman stroked my hair. She didn't say anything. Neither did Papa. Jacqueline began chanting again, but different this time, "No more people, never, never, never . . ."

Papa grabbed her, and tickled her, and she laughed and kicked around until Maman and I yelled for them to stop.

Then Papa got up to make some coffee for Maman and himself. Every Sunday, Papa got up first and made coffee. Maman moved over so that she could be between Jacqueline and me, and each of us could get an equal share of her.

"It's so much better when we don't have anybody else around," I said. "There's never any room to play, and I hate always having to be the last one to use the toilet."

Maman laughed. "You know we have no choice, Nicole. All those poor people, uprooted from their homes because of the Germans. We're so lucky to be living here.

It's the least we can do to help other people in real trouble."

"But why do they have to come *here?*" I asked. "Why can't they go some other place?"

"Where?" Maman asked.

"Anywhere—but not here."

"There is no anywhere left," Maman said. "Germany has conquered just about every country in Europe, except for Switzerland."

"Maman," Jacqueline asked, "will the Germans come here?"

"I hope not, *ma petite.*"

"Say, they won't, Maman, don't just say you hope not."

"I can't say they won't, Jacqueline. I can only hope they won't. But you and Nicole must understand that just because we are safe, and have a home to live in, we must help others who are not so lucky. One day the war will end and—"

"And then nobody will sleep here ever, ever, ever, ever--"

"Jacqueline!"

Later Papa went out for his morning walk. He generally met some friends at the café, and stayed there, talking and drinking coffee until dinnertime.

We had sweet and sour veal stew and peas for dinner. Often now, Maman and Papa traded their sweaters for food instead of money. But their supply was dwindling. They had bought large quantities of sweaters before the war started, but once Paris had been occupied, most of the manufacturers had fled. Some of them now worked in Lyon, but it was becoming harder and harder to get wool or dyes. Most of the sweaters were now made out of synthetic fabrics that were neither warm nor long-lasting. The colors were muddy, and the prices were ridiculous, Papa said. And even these were becoming unavailable.

My parents worked the outdoor markets still, but not every day. There was not enough stock for them to go every day. Maman continued to sew at home whenever she could. I did more and more of the housework and cooking, particularly on the days that my parents were gone.

Maman still complained that I had a big mouth but very often now she was pleased with me.

"Really, Nicole, for a girl your age, you are certainly very capable. Look how you washed all our stockings. And the soup is made, and the table set! There is really nothing you can't do once you make up your mind."

"And me, Maman?" from Jacqueline. "Is there nothing I can't do too? Just like Nicole?"

"Of course not!" from me. "You're only seven, and I'm eleven. Of course you can't do what I can do. You're too little."

"I'm not little, am I, Maman? And I can do anything Nicole can do, can't I?"

"All right, *dinde*. Tomorrow you can do all the shopping, and make the soup for supper."

"I can do it," Jacqueline said, her cheeks a bright red, but not as bright as her long red curls which were trembling across her shoulders.

"We'll see just what you can do," I said. "You don't

even know how to wash the dishes, and when Maman asks you to put away your clothes, you always cry and whine like the big baby you are."

"MAMAN! MAMAN!"

"Nicole," Maman sighs, "there is only one thing, perhaps, you can't do."

"What is it?" I say, hands on my hips, chin out.

"Shut your mouth," Maman says.

After dinner, my parents, Jacqueline, and I walked along the Avenue du Lac. The summer months are the months when the tourists come to Aix-les-Bains, but often September and October are the most beautiful months of the year. This day, the sky was as blue as Jacqueline's eyes, with great, rippling, white puffs of clouds. The air smelled clean and fresh, and there was just enough of a cool breeze on your back to make you feel like walking.

We kept meeting people we knew, many of them, refugees who had stayed with us until they could find places for themselves. Some of them could not find jobs, and Maman said they were living off their savings. I could not understand how they were able to laugh and joke so much. Some of them were separated from members of their family and others had lost almost everything of value. When they came to us, most of them were frightened, upset, sometimes hysterical. But once a few days had passed, they would be laughing and joking as if nothing terrible or unusual had happened.

Here now was M. Henri Bonnet, whose wife had died of an appendicitis attack the day the Germans occupied Paris. So many of the doctors and nurses had left the town, and there was so much confusion that M. Bonnet could find nobody to operate on his wife. And he had left his children with a neighbor who was not there when he returned. Nobody knew where the neighbor had gone or what had happened to the children but everybody told him to get out of Paris since he was Jewish. He thought somebody might have taken the children to his sister in Dijon, so he went there. But the children were not in Dijon, and he could not return to Paris. He wrote letters to everybody he could think of but nobody had seen the children.

"Good day, M. Bonnet."

"Good day, Nicole. Oh, David, I was just on my way over to invite you and Henriette to come to the movie with me tonight. They are showing *La Femme du Boulanger* and it is such an enchanting film. Have you seen it? No? Oh, then you really must. It is absolutely delightful, and Raimu is so funny."

I thought M. Bonnet was disgusting. If Papa and Maman were ever separated from Jacqueline and me, I had no doubt they would be too busy looking for us to go to the movies.

M. Bonnet was laughing so hard, he had to wipe the tears from his eyes. "So then, he finds out what she really thinks of him . . ."

"M. Bonnet," I said, "have you heard any news about your children?"

That made him stop laughing. He blinked a few times, and there was still a tear in one corner of his eye. "No," he said, "nothing."

78

Papa took him by the arm, and they walked on in front of us. Maman took me by the arm too. "What is the matter with you?" she asked. "Have you lost your senses? Why did you torment that poor man like that?" She shook my arm.

"Because he was laughing," I said. "How can he laugh, and go to the movies when his wife died, and his children are lost? If we were lost you and Papa wouldn't laugh, and you wouldn't go to the movies. You'd look for us."

Maman pulled me closer to her, and held me against her for a moment. "Listen, Nicole, M. Bonnet *is* looking for his children, and he *is* grieving. Did you see his face when you asked about them? He is grieving but he has hope that he will find them again. He has lost a great deal, but if human beings can hold on to hope, they can live through the worst of times."

"But you and Papa would look for us. You wouldn't laugh."

"Papa and I would look for you as long as we had any strength left in our bodies, and we would hope for as long as we were alive that we would find you."

"And you wouldn't laugh."

"I think we would. People who don't laugh are dead."

I pulled my arm away, and cried, "If I were separated from you, I would look for you, and that's all I would do. I'd look for you, and I'd find you, and I'd never laugh until I did."

Jacqueline was sobbing. Big tears rolled down her cheeks. "I don't want to be separated from Maman and Papa. You stop that, Nicole. You stop it!"

Maman picked Jacqueline up, and said, "We are not being separated, silly. Nicole and I were just saying if."

"Say we'll never be separated, Maman. Say it! Say never!"

"Of course, *ma poupée,* you know we won't be."

"But say it, Maman, say never, never, never."

"Never," said Maman.

"And I wouldn't laugh," I said, "never, never, never."

Maman began laughing then, and soon Jacqueline buried her head in Maman's shoulder, so we shouldn't see she was laughing, and I laughed too.

We met the Rostens in front of the beach, and they came back to our house for tea. Mme. Rosten said that her cook had left because she felt it was degrading for her to work for Jews.

Dr. Rosten said, "Our Vichy government is a spawning ground for anti-Semitism, and it will get worse, mark my words. Yesterday, one of my patients told me he was going to stop coming to me. He planned on using a Christian doctor. 'Very good, M. Langeron,' I told him, 'and perhaps you will be good enough to pay your bill which I have carried for several years now.' 'Sue me,' he said, and of course he knows a Vichy court will very likely decide in his favor."

"Langeron," murmured Mme. Rosten, taking a tiny sip out of one of Maman's good tea cups. She was wearing a yellow suit, and a brilliant gold and blue scarf. Her small head was covered with short, black curls, each one perfect. "Langeron? Isn't that the man who dragged you out of bed in the middle of the night when his son fell off the roof?"

"The times are getting worse and worse for Jews," her husband said. "Not only in occupied France but here as well. We are no longer safe. Today a Jew can no longer work for the government and a Jewish doctor cannot collect his bills. Tomorrow . . . Why do we stay? What are we waiting for?"

Françoise and I took our tea out on the *veranda*. But I remembered something so I went back into the room.

"Jacqueline," I said, "do you want to come out on the *veranda* with Françoise and me?"

"Me?" Jacqueline was startled.

"Yes, maybe we'll play *Belote.*"

Jacqueline jumped up and came toward me.

"Me too?" asked Monique, Françoise's little sister.

I could hear Françoise groan in back of me.

"Of course, Monique."

We dealt out the cards and began to play. Jacqueline was my partner. I smiled at her, and didn't say one single word when she made stupid moves—and she made many of them. She didn't remember. She never did, but I was always sorry later when I picked on her as I had done this morning.

April 1942

Lucie had been out of school for two days before we heard what had happened.

"It's hard to believe," Papa said. "He seemed such an ordinary, conventional man, even rather stuffy. I never saw him dressed in anything but a suit, and he always carried a cane."

"What, Papa?" Jacqueline asked. "What man?"

"M. Fiori," Papa said. "We are talking about him. A terrible thing has happened. The poor man was arrested three days ago and is being sent back to Italy."

"But why, Papa?" I cried. "What did he do?"

"Nothing," said Maman. "He was a good man, and nowadays it is a crime to be a good man." Her cheeks were pink and her eyes were full of angry lights. "They always seemed so standoffish. And you remember the time their girl called Nicole a Dirty Jew. I didn't realize . . . and now it's too late, and his family is gone too. There is nothing we can do to help."

"Where is his family? Where is Lucie?"

"Nobody knows for sure," Maman said. "Mme. Barras says that Mme. Fiori told Mme. Bonheur that she and the children would go back to Italy with her husband, but then suddenly they disappeared. Mme. Bonheur thinks they were persuaded to go into hiding."

"But what did M. Fiori do?" I asked.

"He was a socialist," Papa said. "He was a leader in the Socialist Party in Italy, and fought against Mussolini. After

85

Mussolini came to power, the Socialist Party was out-lawed, and its leaders were arrested. M. Fiori had to flee or he would have been arrested too. So he came here to France, knowing that he was safe, and that our country would protect him."

"And now," my mother cried, "our country is no better than Italy, and no better than Germany."

"Poor man!" Papa said. "Does anyone know who informed?"

"No, but you can be sure that whoever it was, he will be punished. The underground will find out. They will track him down and . . ."

"What will they do?" asked Jacqueline.

"They will shoot him, of course," I said.

"Of course?" said Papa.

"Yes, of course," said Maman. "And it will serve him right. There is nothing lower or more despicable than an informer."

"But Henriette, did you hear? Your own child talks of shooting as a matter of course."

"David," Maman said, "why don't we go? It doesn't make sense to stay here any more."

"Where would we go?"

"To Switzerland."

"But Henriette, you know this can't last. Now that the United States has entered the war, and the Germans are being pushed back in Russia, it's bound to come to an end. Soon."

"Yes, I know, but I'm afraid."

Papa said, "The important thing is not to panic. In two years, since we lost the war, the Germans have not come here to Aix-les-Bains. They are certainly not going to come now when every soldier they have is needed up north or on the Russian front. The Vichy government, and that senile, old fool, Pétain, will disappear once the war ends. And we will be here where we want to be instead of homeless in some Swiss prison camp."

At school the next day, Mlle. Legrand came into our classroom and spoke to us about what had happened. I was now attending *l'école secondaire,* and in 1941 Mlle. Legrand had become directress. People said she got the post because she was pro-German. There were pictures of Maréchal Pétain hanging in all the classrooms.

She waited while we sang *"La Marseillaise,"* and sat with her head bowed during the moment of silence she had initiated in the past year. In general, most of the girls used the moment of silence to make furtive, funny faces at each other, and there were always stifled giggles which some of the teachers ignored. But this morning, with Mlle. Legrand standing in front of the classroom, there were no funny faces and no laughter.

"I am sure," she said, "you have all heard about what has happened to Lucie Fiori's family. It is impossible for us not to feel sad at the loss of a classmate, and to hope and pray that she will be safe wherever she is."

Mlle. Legrand lowered her head again, and several of the girls in the class who were friends of Lucie's did the same. You could see their lips moving as they prayed.

"It is sad," said Mlle. Legrand, "that the innocent must always suffer along with the guilty. In some cases, the guilty do not suffer at all.

"Today in France, it is you and me, and other innocents who are suffering not only from physical hardships—these are unimportant. You may not have as much to eat as you would like, but none of you is starving. And even if you were, that would be preferable to being starved spiritually and morally.

"Which is why France is suffering and bleeding today. Because evil, little, grasping men have brought our country to its knees. Men who have thought only of material needs, and not of their country's honor. Men who have no morality, no religion, no ideals.

"What a spectacle France has been in the eyes of the world, as one clamorous, mewling republic after another has tottered and fallen. Our poor torn country has been yearning for a strong leader who would restore sanity and order. And now we have him. His name, as you all know, is M. le Maréchal Henri Pétain.

In front of me, Marie and Georgette were looking at each other. Marie's eyebrows were raised just a little bit, and Georgette wrinkled up her nose as if something smelled bad. I supposed that their families felt the same way about Maréchal Pétain as mine.

"His wisdom and courage," Mlle. Legrand said, "have helped us bear the humiliation of France's defeat. He has helped us to understand that Germany is not our enemy, and Italy is not our enemy. Our enemy is the rottenness here in our own midst which must be ruthlessly cut out. We must cleanse ourselves of the political agitators, the godless troublemakers who have weakened France in the past, and will destroy her completely unless they are eliminated.

"We must all, you and I—but particularly you, for you are the future—pledge ourselves to forge a new France, a strong and glorious one. We must obey our leader, Maréchal Pétain, without question, and we must bear without complaint any little sacrifices he asks of us. We must also understand that if some measures our government takes seem harsh, they are necessary to cleanse our country of weakness, and to restore her to her former place of greatness and glory among the nations of the world."

I stood in front of Lucie's house that day after school and looked at the dust and specks of dirt that lay on the stairs. For three days Mme. Fiori had not swept. There was nobody in the house. I knew it, and yet as I climbed the stairs I felt as if I was being watched. I had never been so close to that door before, and I could feel my heart beating high up in my throat, and behind my ears.

I put my hand on the doorknob, and turned. But it was locked. Lucie was gone, and now there was no chance that her door would ever open for me.

It was me screaming that night, not Jacqueline. Me, who Maman was rocking in her arms, chanting, "Shh, shh, *ma poupée,* shh, shh, what is it?"

"Oh, Maman," I wept, "she's gone now and she'll never be back."

"Who, *chérie?* Who is gone?"

"Lucie Fiori. I'll never see her again. Never, never, Maman. How can I bear it?"

"Shh, perhaps you will, Nicole. We must hope that the war will end soon."

"Maman, why did she hate me so much? I always

liked her, and tried to be her friend. And now, there will never be a chance for us to be friends, will there, Maman?"

Maman kissed my forehead and held me tighter in her arms. "Of course there is a chance. There is always a chance. Once the war is over, no doubt the Fioris will return. And we will plan a big party for them."

"But Lucie will not want to come."

"Yes, yes, she will come. I myself will invite her, and you know, Nicole, I won't let her say no to me."

"That's right, Maman, and once she comes here, and sits awhile with me on the *veranda,* and we talk and maybe play *Aux Dames* or *Belote,* she will see that I'm not so bad as she thinks."

"Yes, I'm sure she will become your friend once she gets to know you."

"Do you really think so, Maman?"

"Yes, I really do, Nicole. And now do you think you can sleep again? Look how Jacqueline has slept through everything."

"I think I can sleep now, Maman, but come and sit here for just a few minutes more, and talk to me about the party. What kind of food will we serve?"

That April we celebrated Passover. I had never been to a seder before, and neither had Françoise. It was to be at her house because there would be thirty-two guests, but my father would conduct the seder.

There were two tables in the dining room with thirty-two chairs, and still there was room to walk around. Each table had bowls of fresh flowers, tall silver candlesticks, gleaming wine glasses, and gold-rimmed china plates that all matched. Even the children had wine glasses and gold-rimmed china plates.

On each table was a platter containing the symbols of Passover—matzoh (unleavened bread), marror (bitter herbs), haroseth (a paste made of chopped apples, nuts, cinnamon, and wine), the shank bone of a lamb, a roasted egg, and parsley. Next to the platter was a dish of salted water.

Papa explained that Passover is a holiday which celebrates freedom. It is a very ancient holiday, going back to the time when the Jews were the slaves of the Egyptians. Moses was the leader who led the Jews out of Egypt to freedom. Each of the foods on the platter had a meaning, Papa said. The matzoh is the flat bread which the Jews ate after they fled in the night from Egypt. There had been no time for them to wait for their bread to rise. The bitter herbs symbolize the bitterness of slavery. Haroseth represents the mortar that the Jews used in making bricks for their Egyptian masters. The shank bone stands for God's mighty arm, and the egg is an allusion to his love and kindness. The parsley symbolizes the rebirth of all things, including hope, and the salt water represents the Red Sea which our ancestors crossed over in their flight out of Egypt.

Each of the men wore yarmulkas on their heads. Dr. Rosten had a new white one, and he laughed and said he had never worn one in his entire life. He had never been inside a synagogue, he said, and of course had never been to a seder. He had read over the *Haggadah* my father had given him, and would do the best he could to follow along during the ceremony.

Papa's yarmulka was an old one which he said had belonged to his grandfather. It was made of blue velvet with gold embroidery.

"It's ironic, isn't it?" Dr. Rosten said to Papa. "I never knew I was a Jew until Hitler surfaced, and my wife's family was even more remote. Her great-great-great-grandfather was an adviser to Napoleon, a colonel in his army, and one of the first to be killed in the Russian campaign. We have always been sure of being French but not at all sure of being Jewish. Now, suddenly, we are sure of being Jewish, and not at all sure of being French."

"And I," said Papa, "was trained as a Jew, and tried to forget it, but that too was impossible."

Even though Mme. Rosten had a cook—a Jewish one now—most of the women guests were busy in the kitchen, helping to arrange the food in large bowls and platters. The smells of these and the roasting chickens were overpowering. I had not seen so much food in one place for a long, long time.

"Carrots," one of the guests was saying to Mme. Rosten, "are so expensive, I don't think I've eaten any for ages . . . and leeks! . . . where did you ever find leeks?"

Françoise and I helped carry the food out to the table, but it was difficult with all the younger children underfoot.

It was time to begin. The candles were lit, and my father recited the kiddush in Hebrew, blessing the wine. Then he at his table and Dr. Rosten at ours divided up the symbolic food so that each of us had a taste—the bitter with the sweet.

At first, everybody was quiet as my father began the

long service which told the story of Passover. After a while, the younger children began squirming and then giggling, and even I found myself waiting for the talking to end and the eating to begin. I think my father skipped some portions because it wasn't too long before all of us were singing the Had Gadyah.

"The one kid, the one kid, that my father bought for two
    zuzim, the one kid
And the cat came and ate the kid that my father bought
    for two zuzim, the one kid
And the dog came, and bit the cat that ate the kid that my
    father bought for two zuzim, the one kid
And the stick came and beat the dog that bit the cat that
    ate the kid, etc.
And the fire came and burned the stick that beat the dog,
    etc.
And the water came and put out the fire that burned the
    stick, etc.
And the ox came and drank up the water that put out the
    fire, etc.
And the butcher came and butchered the ox that drank up
    the water, etc.
And the Angel of Death came and slaughtered the butcher
    who butchered the ox, etc.
And the Holy One, blessed be He, came and slaughtered
    the Angel of Death, who slaughtered the butcher, who
    butchered the ox, who drank up the water that put
    out the fire, that burned the stick, that beat the dog,
    that bit the cat, that ate the kid, that my father bought
    for two zuzim, the one kid, the one kid."

The food was so good, I didn't start talking until the soup when I said to Françoise, "You know that song we sang, the Had Gadyah? My father said that the kid stood for the Jewish people, and all the animals and people and things that hurt the kid are the countries like Assyria and Babylonia and Persia who used to persecute the Jews in the ancient world. At the end, all of them are destroyed."

Françoise blew on a spoonful of soup. She put it into her mouth and swallowed, then she turned toward me. "Yes," she said, "but the kid is destroyed too, so what good is it?"

"No, no," I said. "You are wrong. The kid is not destroyed. It can't be, otherwise we wouldn't all be sitting around here arguing about it."

"Don't be silly," Françoise said. "Of course it's destroyed. The cat eats the kid, isn't that right?"

"Yes."

"So that's the end of the kid, no?"

"No. Because maybe the cat swallows the kid whole, and somehow or other, when they're all busy killing one another, the kid manages to come out of it alive. I think he is maybe a little bit weak at first, and probably he doesn't stand up straight for a while, and I think he must wobble when he finally does walk. But he doesn't die. He can't die."

Françoise reached out for another piece of matzoh.

"Françoise?" I said.

"What?"

"Well, what do you think?"

"I think," said Françoise, "that you should eat your soup. It's getting cold."

September 1943

THE GERMANS occupied Aix-les-Bains in June of 1943. Most people expected them because of the allied victories in North Africa, and the threat of an allied invasion through Italy. Most people said that, in spite of Maréchal Pétain's assurances, the Germans would take over unoccupied France. My father said they would not come. He believed that when the invasion took place it would be through western France and not Italy. All through the winter, as one town after another was occupied by German troops, my father said they would never come to Aix-les-Bains.

One day they were suddenly, quietly there. We saw German nurses walking together along the Rue de Genève. Like the summer tourists, they laughed and talked and acted as if they belonged here. There were no parades, no tanks, no banners as we had expected. We saw very few soldiers—a couple of officers sitting at the café, and politely moving their chairs to allow other people to pass, a few of the soldiers, in their gray-green uniforms with cameras in front of the Arc de Campanus.

"It's unreal," Maman said. "They wipe out towns, kill hostages, imprison, torture, burn . . . But here, they enter the town like tourists, and everybody acts as if it's all very ordinary. For two days we all stay in, but now nobody seems to notice they're even around."

"We're not important," Papa said. "Thank God!

There's just a small force stationed here. They don't have the strength to do anything. They're harmless."

"Last week in Les Beauges," Maman said, "they shot three members of the underground, and also the family that was hiding them. How can you say that they're harmless?"

Maman talked all the time now about leaving France. She wanted to go to Annemasse and pay a runner to sneak us across the border into Switzerland. Papa said it was too dangerous. Maman said that staying in Aix-les-Bains and waiting for the Germans to come and get us was not only more dangerous, it was stupid as well. Papa said people got shot crossing the border illegally, and even if you did get over, and the Swiss Guards didn't send you back, then they would put you in a prison camp where you'd probably starve to death or die of the cold before the war ended.

"It's the only chance we have," Maman said. "At least we will be safe in Switzerland, and not be treated differently from any other refugees just because we're Jewish."

Every day now, people we knew were leaving for Switzerland. Even M. Bonnet had gone weeks ago.

"Now he will never find his children," I said to Maman.

"Yes he will," said Maman. "He has a much better chance of finding them if he is alive to look for them, and he will remain alive in Switzerland."

Papa said it didn't make sense to go to Switzerland. He said the Germans were losing. It was only a matter of time. To leave France would be to give up everything. Perhaps it would be impossible to get back again. And then, we had so many good friends in the town. Even if the Germans were planning a roundup of the Jews, he was positive that we would hear about it beforehand and have plenty of time to go into hiding.

Maman talked about leaving all the time now. The business was dead, and my father had stopped going to the markets. Maman still sewed at home but there was hardly any money coming in, and even if there was, there was not much to buy—bad bread, synthetic coffee, hardly any meat or cheese, no eggs, no potatoes, very few fruits or vegetables. Everything was rationed—clothing as well as food.

My parents argued every day now. Their voices grew hard and angry. Even Jacqueline's tears did not make them stop.

"Mme. Labarthe heard from her brother and his family, and now she will be leaving in a few days. They are in a detention camp, but people are kind to them. There is a school for the children, and the Red Cross and other organizations bring them extra food and clothing. There was no problem crossing the border. Mme. Labarthe says the guards usually look the other way."

"And what will happen when they come back, if they come back?"

"They will worry about it then."

"I am not going to drag my family out in the middle of the night, and run the danger of having them shot."

Jacqueline started crying. Papa picked her up, and held her very tight. "My God, do you think I could stand it if anything happened to any one of you?"

"Something will certainly happen to all of us, if we don't get out now."

"Leave me be!" my father shouted. "You never stop. I can't stand it!"

Some nights now, Papa went to the café and stayed there with the men, drinking and playing cards. Maman cried, and waited up for him, and they would argue when he came home. Many times I had to hold Jacqueline in my arms and tell her stories. She was afraid of being put into a prison camp in Switzerland, and she did not want to go.

One night when Papa was out, and Maman was crying in her bedroom, I got out of bed, dressed, and tiptoed out of the apartment. Down in the street I met my father coming toward me. He was looking at me but didn't seem to know who I was until I said, "Papa" and put my hand on his arm.

"Nicole?"

"Yes, Papa. Please come home now. Maman is crying."

"But Nicole, you shouldn't be out on the streets at night. It's dangerous."

"It's dangerous for you too, Papa, and you shouldn't drink all that wine. You will feel sick tomorrow."

"I know, I know," my father said.

He put his arm on my shoulder, and I helped him home.

A few days later, at breakfast, Maman had a smile all over her face. She looked fresh and happy and said she had some good news for us.

"What is it, Maman?"

"Papa has decided that he will go to Switzerland. He will make sure it is safe, and once he gets over he will send word to us, and we will join him."

"I don't want to go to Switzerland," Jacqueline cried. "They will put me in prison, and I don't want to be put in prison. I want to stay here."

"It will only be for a little while," I told Jacqueline, "until the war is over. You can take your doll with you, and once we are there, I will show you how to make a beaded purse for her."

"Really? But every time I ask you now, you always say you have no time."

"Yes, but once we are in Switzerland, I promise I will show you how."

Maman nodded at me approvingly. "You are really growing up, Nicole," she said.

"I *am* thirteen, Maman."

"Yes," said Maman, and she looked me up and down as if she was seeing me for the first time.

Papa was going to take the train to Annemasse on Thursday afternoon. In Annemasse, he would go to a certain address where he would meet the runner, and any other people who were planning to cross the border. He carried a small suitcase, and if anyone questioned him, he would say that he was visiting a relative.

Nobody questioned him. I went down to the station with him, but Maman and Jacqueline stayed at home so that it would not look suspicious.

There were two German soldiers in the station who were waiting to take the train. One of them was eating chocolate, and I could feel my stomach ache with longing. It had been so long since I had tasted chocolate. I watched him as he ate it, quickly, talking to his friend all the time, and hardly noticing what he was eating. "Slow down," I wanted to say. "Don't eat it so fast. Let me watch you." A few crumbs scattered on his jacket, and he brushed them away with his hand.

Papa held his suitcase slightly behind him as he walked through the station house. But the soldiers never looked our way at all.

The train was due in a few minutes. Papa and I walked up and down the station platform while we waited.

"As soon as I can," Papa said, "I'll get word to you, and if I consider it safe then the three of you will come."

"Yes, Papa."

"And Nicole, Maman will have a lot to do while I'm gone, and I want you to promise that you will help her, and do everything she asks."

"I promise, Papa."

He put his free hand on my shoulder and said, "You're a good girl, Nicole, and you're really growing up."

"I'm thirteen, Papa."

"Yes, I know, but even for thirteen you are extremely capable, and very mature."

I didn't say anything. What can you say when you hear something like that?

"I don't feel so bad about leaving when I know Maman has you to depend on."

I remained silent.

"And Nicole . . ."

"Yes, Papa?"

"Nicole . . . just in case you don't hear from me . . ."

"But we will, Papa. You won't have any trouble getting a letter to us. M. Bonnet and the Simons wrote letters, and so did many of the others who went."

"Yes, of course I won't have any trouble," Papa said, "but just in case . . ."

I waited.

"Just in case . . ."

"We will come looking for you, Papa. Don't worry! And we will find you."

"No!" said Papa. "If you don't hear from me, I don't want you to come. I want you to . . ."

"To what, Papa?"

"I don't know," my father said. We could hear the train approaching, and the other passengers came out onto the platform. The two German soldiers walked in our direction. One of them was combing his long, blond hair with a black pocket comb. They passed us, and Papa said, "Why am I going? How can I go? What kind of a man am I to go away and leave my family here?"

"Papa," I urged, "it will only be for a short time."

"No," said Papa. "Look at Henri Bonnet. No!" He put his suitcase down on the ground. "I'm not going. It doesn't make sense. And besides, we're making it all much worse than it really is. All those crazy stories! Who can believe them?"

He turned to look at the two German soldiers who were about to board the train. "A few more months and it will be over. You heard the BBC broadcast the other night. The Allies are already in Italy. For a few more months, why should I go? Nothing will happen in our town."

"Papa," I said, "Maman will be disappointed."

But he stood there, and I stood next to him. After a while, the train pulled out of the station, and he picked up his suitcase and said, "Let's go home."

Maman cried when she saw him, but she kissed him, and hugged him, and she kissed me, and I kissed her, and Jacqueline kissed Papa, and then we were all kissing and nobody really felt sorry that my father hadn't gone.

After that, Maman never spoke about going to Switzerland.

November 1943

SWITZERLAND

1943

Françoise
Rosten

THAT LAST NIGHT the Rostens came to say good-bye. Earlier in the day, Maman handed me one of the last of her stock of sweaters, and two pairs of cotton stockings, and told me to take them out to the Blanchards.

They had a farm about ten kilometers outside of Aix-les-Bains, ordinarily a short, pleasant ride on my bicycle. But on that day, there was a wind blowing against my face all the way there, and I had to pedal hard to make progress. I was out of breath when I arrived, and Mme. Blanchard gave me a glass of water, and told me to rest a few minutes before biking back.

She was pleased with the sweater. She asked me to tell Maman that if she had any gloves or hats, she could use some of them, too.

Then she went off and after a while came back with a chicken and a bag with four or five potatoes. She helped me put the food in my bicycle bag and cover it with the old school books I always carried just in case I was stopped.

I was about to leave when Mme. Blanchard hesitated, and said, "Just a minute, Nicole." She headed off to the chicken coop and in a few minutes came back, carrying two eggs.

"Eggs! Mme. Blanchard, we haven't had eggs for so long I can hardly remember what they taste like."

She began complaining how the Germans took everything, and that she and her family had barely enough to
eat for themselves. She said that the hens hardly laid any
more, and even if they did, she was supposed to turn all
the eggs over to the Germans, so she never ate eggs either.
I nodded sympathetically, even though I was pretty sure
that there were secret places throughout the farm with
more food hidden than I could bear thinking about.

On the way back I passed a patrol of four German
soldiers riding around in an open car. If they found the
food in my bag I knew I would be in trouble. But it
wasn't the first time I had ridden out to the farm on such
an errand, and I had never been searched or even stopped
before. I moved discreetly over to the other side of the
road and passed the car, my eyes down. But I could hear
the car stopping, and in a moment a voice behind me
shouted in French, "You!"

My heart beat fast in my throat, and I was frightened.
I stopped my bike and turned my head. "Me, Monsieur?"

"Yes, you." There was some laughter, and then, "Come
here!"

I laid the bicycle down on the side of the road, and
walked slowly toward them. The road was quite empty,
and it was beginning to rain. I stopped about three or
four feet from the car, and the driver said, "Come here!"

On both sides of the road were fields that were fenced
in. But a little to the right of the Germans' car, I noted
that the fence was missing a bottom piece. If it proved
necessary, I could squeeze through the opening there, and

run while they would have to climb over. Of course, if they had guns . . .

I moved a little closer.

"What is your name?"

"Nicole Nieman."

"How old are you?"

"Eleven, Monsieur."

Which was not true, of course. But on a deserted country road, with four German soldiers looking at me, I thought it was wiser to take advantage of the fact that I was small for my age.

One of the soldiers snorted and said something in German. The driver started up the car, and without another word they were off. That was the first time I ever spoke to a German soldier.

Maman boiled the eggs for Jacqueline and me. It had been a long time, six months or more since I had eaten an egg, and it was like discovering an entirely new food.

My mother listened to my account of the meeting with the German patrol. She shook her head and said, "You handled that very well, Nicole. I am proud of you. But I think from now on we won't have you go alone out to the farm."

"But why not, Maman? The Germans didn't even ask me what I had in my bicycle bag. They never ask children."

"Maybe so, but I don't want you biking out in the country by yourself any more. Only if Papa or I or some other adult is along."

"But Maman, I can look after myself."

Maman exploded. "You do what I tell you, Nicole! Do you hear?"

I turned my face away and refused to answer. She took my arm and shook it. "Do you hear?"

"Yes, I hear." I pulled my arm away and started to leave the room.

Maman said quietly—her cheeks were still red but her voice had no anger in it—"I know you can look after yourself, but thank goodness you don't have to—yet. One day, I hope, when you are a little older, you will look after yourself, and I know you will be able to do it. But not yet."

I ran out of the room and sulked on the *veranda* until I remembered that tonight the Rostens were coming to say good-bye, and after that I would not see Françoise again.

"Maman," I cried, running into the kitchen, "may I spend the rest of the afternoon with Françoise?"

She was sitting at the kitchen table, plucking the chicken, and she started shaking her head, but then she stopped and said, "It's all right with me if Mme. Rosten doesn't mind. They will be busy getting things in order, but if she doesn't think you are in the way you may stay until all of you come back for supper."

"Do you need me to help?"

"Mmm . . ." Maman looked around the kitchen and said, "That's all right. Today Jacqueline will help. After all, she is nine years old and is also very capable."

I kept my doubts on that score to myself and hurried off to Françoise.

You would have thought that this being their last day in Aix-les-Bains, everything would be upside down, and Mme. Rosten would be tearing around, her clothes somewhat creased, her hair disarranged. But no, she was seated at her desk in the downstairs study, writing letters. She was wearing a soft white blouse, and her shining dark, curly hair was all in place.

Mme. Rosten had a way of wearing blouses that I had tried to copy ever since I met her. Her blouse always stayed tucked in at her skirt, and if she wore a sweater, a tiny edge of her sleeve always showed, crisp and neat below the sweater cuff. I wore blouses too—almost every day, as did most of the girls in my class. But my blouses became rumpled and never stayed in place. Françoise had the same cool, unrumpled look as her mother. Both of them could wear the simplest clothes and look more elegant than someone dressed in the height of fashion. It was this look that I strove for and never attained.

Everything looked the same in their house. They were taking nothing with them. Tomorrow morning Dr. Rosten would leave first, just as he did every morning, on his way to see his patients. But he would not see any patients. Instead, he would take the train to Annemasse and wait for his wife and children. Later in the morning, Mme. Rosten, Françoise, and Monique, with one small suitcase between them, would also take the train, and meet Dr. Rosten that same evening. Hopefully, by the following day they would be in Switzerland.

Dr. Rosten brought a few apples and a small piece of Brie cheese to supper that night. Maman had bowls of chicken stew for everybody, and by eating slowly and taking small bites and chewing more times than was really necessary, it was enough.

Papa was cheerful. He listened to the BBC broadcasts almost every night now in his bedroom with the curtains drawn. The Germans were losing ground every day now in Russia, the Allies were advancing in Italy, and Mussolini had already fallen.

"A matter of months," he said. "By spring or summer at the latest, it will be over."

"I hope you're right," said Dr. Rosten, "but still I think you would be wise to leave."

"Why?" said my father. "We can manage until the end. The Germans have been here five months and it is no worse than it was before. They would not dare to bother us. They know as well as we do that the end is in sight."

"Yet in Paris we know that they continue to round up Jews, and in—"

"Paris! Paris!" my father said impatiently. "We are not Paris. Nothing will happen here. Nothing ever happens here."

Mme. Rosten brought Maman a present, a beautiful cut-glass pitcher that was unbelievably heavy. She said that after the war, when they returned to France, their family would live in Paris. She had always believed the country was the proper place for children to grow up which was why they had moved to Aix-les-Bains. Once the war ended, however, Françoise and Monique would be old enough to go to boarding school in Switzerland, and she hungered for all the cultural advantages Paris offered.

Françoise cried out, "But then I won't see Nicole again. Maman, I don't want to go away to boarding school."

Mme. Rosten said not to forget all the school holidays and the summer holidays. She said I could come and spend all my free time with Françoise in Paris. She would show me the Louvre, and take me to the theater, and we would have tea at La Marquise de Sévigné off the Champs Élysées.

"I always wanted to see Paris," I said. "Maman and Papa promised when I was older they would take me with them on one of their business trips, but then the war started, and I never went."

"Well then, once the war is over, and we are back, your parents can bring you up with them, and you and Françoise will spend a long, long holiday together."

"And if Mme. Duclos, the dressmaker, is still in business," Maman said, "I will take you over to see her, Nicole, and she will make you a beautiful dress. She is very expensive, but nobody can do the kind of embroidery she does, or add the special. little scallops on the hems."

Mme. Rosten was interested. "What is her name? Where did you say she had her shop? Let me write it down, and I will certainly look her up."

"There was a green dress she made for a customer— you see, I worked for her when I first came to France, but I never could do the kind of work she did—with beads and embroidered flowers around the neck. I have never forgotten that dress. She offered to make my wedding dress when I married David, but there was no time. And so she said she would make me a dress as a weding present any time I wanted one. So many years have passed, and I never asked her for it, but she is still working—at least, last time I was in Paris she was—and so once the war is over I will take Nicole to Paris and introduce her to Mme. Duclos and say, " 'Now I am ready for my wedding present.' "

Maman giggled like a young girl.

"But, Maman, will she do it?" I cried. "Will she remember?"

"Of course, she will remember."

"And, Maman, I want a green dress just like the one you described, with flowers and beads around the neck."

Mme. Rosten said she thought I should have a white dress embroidered with pearls and silver thread around the neck. Or perhaps a pale yellow one with pale blue and gold embroidery.

"I will go along with you," said Mme. Rosten, "and we will talk it over with the dressmaker. Nicole has such lovely dark hair and eyes. I do think white or yellow would be perfect for her."

"Maman," said Jacqueline, "will I have a dress too?"

"Of course," Maman laughed, pulling Jacqueline against her. "When you are older, we will have Mme. Duclos make a dress for you too."

"But Maman," Jacqueline said, a worried look on her face, "Mme. Duclos only promised you one dress."

"Yes, yes," Maman laughed, "but after the war we will work very hard and become very rich, and there will be enough money by the time you are thirteen or fourteen for you to have a dress too."

All of us spoke and laughed a lot that night. We would not be seeing the Rostens again until after the war ended. Nobody spoke of the separation, but when it was time to go, Françoise and I clung to each other, and both of us wept. Mme. Rosten invited me to come home with them and spend the night with Françoise. She said I could go on to school from their house in the morning. Maman agreed, and I hurried to get my schoolbooks and pajamas. The grownups lingered on the landing outside our door.

Once I had gathered my things together, I joined Françoise on the staircase below the landing. We waited for the grownups to finish talking. Finally we heard Mme. Rosten murmur, *"Au revoir,"* and begin to move toward the staircase. I remembered that in the excitement I had forgotten to kiss my parents good night, and I turned, looking for my mother on the landing. But she was not there, and I saw the Rostens moving toward me, down the staircase. The wedge of light that flowed out of our apartment into the dark hall narrowed until it was gone. I could hear the door shut. Then I turned and followed Françoise down into the street, happy to be with her.

November 1943

I WAS WEARING Françoise's little gold ring with the initials FR carved on it when I came home for dinner at noon the next day. Before I left for school, she and I had exchanged gifts. I gave her my most precious thing— the locket Papa had made for me. It had his and Maman's picture inside it, and Françoise said she would leave it that way. Wearing it would make her feel like me.

All morning at school I was eager to get home and show Maman the ring. I was feeling guilty about parting with Papa's locket but I hoped he would understand.

Jacqueline was not at school that morning. Another one of her mysterious sore throats, I thought. Between Jacqueline's sore throats and her dislike of school, she managed to stay home on many days. It did not seem surprising to me then that she was absent. What did seem surprising, and painful, was the sight of Françoise's empty seat.

Nobody was home. The kitchen was perfectly neat with no traces of the preparations for last night's supper party. Maman must have stayed up late, cleaning.

But right in the middle of the living room floor lay the cut-glass pitcher that Mme. Rosten had given to Maman. Only its handle was intact. The rest had shattered in hundreds of tiny, sharp fragments.

What could have happened? Perhaps Jacqueline had knocked over the pitcher and cut herself so badly that there was no time to clean up. Perhaps Maman had rushed her off to the hospital.

I hurried out to the *veranda,* and looked up and down the street. Neither of them was in sight but nothing was out of place. Some of the stragglers from school were still walking home for dinner. Across the street, Mme. Claude was washing her windows, and you could clearly hear the sounds of laughter and conversations from passers-by. I felt comforted as I usually did on the *veranda,* and I sat down and began to wonder what I should do next. Perhaps Mme. Barras, our landlady, who lived downstairs and knew everything that happened to everybody on our street could tell me.

I headed back through the apartment. The door to my parents' bedroom was open. Nothing was in place there. Every drawer in their chest had been pulled out. Papers lay scattered all over the room. My mother's coat with the fur collar lay on the floor—hats, jackets, dresses, and sweaters twisted together in a pile on their bed. On top of the whole thing lay our family's photograph album with some of the pages torn out.

All I could think of doing was to put those pages back in place. I picked one up—it was of Jacqueline when she was a year old. There were four pictures of her on the page, and one of them had come loose from its hinges and was hanging at a crazy angle.

"Nicole! Nicole!" somebody said behind me. It was Mme. Barras. She had both hands cradling her face and was rocking it back and forth.

"What happened?" I cried. "Where's my mother and Jacqueline?"

"Nicole," said Mme. Barras, "you have to get away. You can't stay here. They were looking for you too. How lucky you were that you were not home. But go now! Don't stay! They are coming back."

"What happened?" I cried again.

"The Germans. They came. Last night. First they knocked at my door. It was late—maybe two or three in the morning. Two of them came in, and two stayed outside in the car. 'Where are the Jews?' they asked me. 'I don't know,' I told them. 'I don't know about any Jews.' 'Where are the Niemans? We are looking for them. Take us up to their apartment.' What could I do, Nicole?" Mme. Barras was crying now. "They pushed me up the stairs ahead of them, and they began banging on the door. Your father opened the door, and they pushed him out of the way, and came inside. Ah, Nicole, Nicole! Your poor mother! She got down on her hands and knees to those animals. She begged them to take her and leave Jacqueline and your father, but they kept asking where you were. Finally your father said you were staying with friends in Chambéry. Then the Germans arrested them and told them to take only a few clothes. One of the Germans asked for money, and began looking through all their things. But the other said to wait, and they would come back later. Don't stay here, Nicole. They are coming back. Hurry! Go away!"

"But where are my parents? Where did they take them?"

"I don't know, but you must go and hide someplace before they catch you too."

"Where should I go? Where can I hide? Perhaps in the cellar?"

"No, you can't stay here! They will be back, and will certainly search the whole house. They warned me not to let any more Jews live in my house again or I would be arrested too. It's not safe, Nicole. You must go now!"

She was pulling my arm, and I reached out and grabbed the album of pictures and ran down the stairs. I was frightened and my panic made it hard for me to breathe. My bicycle was leaning against the outside of the building. I dropped the album into my bag and then leaped onto the seat.

"Nicole! Nicole!" from across the street. It was Mme. Claude, washing her windows, twisting on the ledge to see me. "Nicole!" It was a whispered cry that could be heard up and down the street. "Run, Nicole! They are looking for you. Run!"

Stiff with terror, I rode away from that street. What brought me to Berthe and Isaac's place, I don't know. They lived in a small apartment behind a cabinetmaker's shop. There was an entrance through the store, and one through an outside alley. I rode my bike through the alley and leaped off, pounded on their door, and cried, "Berthe! Isaac! Berthe! Isaac!" over and over again. No one answered. The door was locked. I looked through the window which was on street level, and saw the clothes and papers scattered on the floor, and one chair turned upside down.

I must have laid there on the ground, crying, for more than an hour. Gradually I became aware of the sound of

the cabinetmaker's hammer. There were other sounds—
pots and pans rattling in an upstairs kitchen, and a
woman singing. Nobody heard me.

The terror had gone. I began to think. Where could I
go where I would be safe, and where I could find out
about my parents and help them? Who knows how many
Jews had been rounded up last night. It would be point-
less for me to try to find out. Where should I go then?
My parents had friends in town who were not Jewish.
Which one of them should I appeal to?

None, I finally decided. I got on my bike and began
pedaling. I would go to the Durands. They lived about
five kilometers out of town, far enough away for me to
be safe, but not so far that M. Durand could not find out
where my parents had been taken.

I knew they would help me. Even though we had been
away from them for five years, Jacqueline and I still
visited them several times a year, and each time Mme.
Durand called us her girls, and said how tall and beautiful
both of us were growing. Even Hitler became crazy whenever we came, leaping all over Jacqueline and licking her
with his long, rough tongue.

They were kind to me that night. Mme. Durand filled
me full of hot soup, and held my hand, and promised
that they would help. I must not worry, said M. Durand.
He would go into town first thing tomorrow, find out
what had happened, and see what he could do to set mat-
ters straight.

That night Mme. Durand put me to sleep in the little
room Jacqueline and I used to share. She sat there on the

side of the bed and chatted about how Célestin had fallen off his bike and broken his elbow a few months ago, and how Jean-Pierre was growing so fast, none of his clothes fit him for more than a few months. Nothing seemed real to me except for the soft bed and the warm feather comforter. I fell asleep.

M. Durand was gone when I woke in the morning. The boys had already left for school. I stayed with Mme. Durand all day, helping her cook and clean. I stayed close to her, comforted by her familiar warm, sweaty smell. She assured me many times that day that she was like a second mother to me, and that until my parents returned, her home was my home.

M. Durand returned in the middle of the afternoon. Twelve Jewish families, he said, had been rounded up that first night my parents were taken, and five more last night. Most of the Jews left in town, he understood, were now in hiding. He had not been able to find out where my parents and the other prisoners were taken. Perhaps they had already left town, headed possibly for Drancy, the prison camp outside of Paris.

But it was not safe to ask too many questions now. Perhaps in a week or so he could go back and make further inquiries. The Germans were instituting a general reign of terror. He was told that not only Jews were being arrested, but others too. Christians—who were suspected of having ties with the underground or those who hid Jews wanted by the Germans. Christians were being arrested—and all their family with them—children too.

Next morning M. and Mme. Durand told me I could

not stay with them. It was not safe for me, they said, since the Germans would certainly be out their way looking for me. M. Durand said he had an old uncle, a widower without children, who lived out in the country near Gap. He had decided that the safest thing, for me, would be to stay with his uncle or with somebody else in that area. Later that afternoon, he said he would take me out to his uncle and make all the necessary arrangements.

"No," I said, "I don't want to go."

"But why not, Nicole? You will be safe in Gap."

"It is too far away. I want to be here when my parents return."

"We will be on the lookout for them, and we will tell them where you are."

"Why can't I stay here?"

"It's not safe."

"I could stay in the little cellar room behind the closet. Nobody would ever think of looking there."

"Impossible. You must do what we say now, Nicole. It is not safe for you to stay here."

"Not safe for whom?" I asked, and then I was sorry I said it. Nobody answered me. A little later, when both of them were not looking, I left the house, got on my bicycle, and rode back to Aix-les-Bains.

There was a lock on our apartment door, and when I asked, Mme. Barras said the Germans had put it there, and she did not have the key. She asked me to go, and closed the door.

I went to the house of M. and Mme. Bernard, friends of my parents. It seemed to me there was a fluttering of the curtains when I knocked at the door but nobody answered.

There was no one at M. Henri's house, and the baker who had a shop downstairs said he thought they had gone to visit their married daughter in Annecy.

Mme. Latour opened the door when I knocked but did not let me in. She said she was a sick woman, and M. Latour had a bad heart. She said I should go and ask the Henris to help me.

"But I have gone there, Madame, and they are not at home."

"Try again later," she said, and shut the door.

All day I rode my bike through the town but there was no place to go. I passed the Rostens' house but did not stop. I did not know until weeks later that they had found their way safely to Switzerland. Then I was afraid of what I might see if I looked through their windows. The day was warm and clear but as night came the temperatures dropped. I saw children playing, men hurrying home from work, women with bundles in their arms. I rode all over town, and everything seemed as it had always seemed. Nothing had changed. Only I was no longer a part of it.

I had eaten nothing since breakfast. I had no money to buy food. I was tired, hungry, and so cold that I believed if I stopped bicycling I would freeze to death. There was a blank in my mind about where to go and what to do. I only knew that I would not go back to the Durands whatever happened. I would not leave town. I would not lose my parents like M. Bonnet's children. I would look after myself until they returned to me.

As long as I could, I bicycled, past the baths, the park, the Arc de Campanus, along the lake, the Palais de Savoie . . . It seemed finally that nothing else moved that night except for me.

On the Rue de Sévigné, a half block from my school, I could go no farther. I dragged myself to the entrance and huddled against the door. I knew that the building was locked and empty at this hour, but there was no place else for me to go.

I woke and slept, woke and slept, woke and slept all through the night. There were warm and happy dreams that I awoke from with my teeth chattering and the tears still wet on my face. I drifted back and forth from cold to warm, from despair to joy. It was an endless night with dreams that finally became all beginnings and ends, and a cold that grew to be a part of myself.

Mlle. Legrand found me there in the morning and pulled me inside the building.

"My poor Nicole," she said, embracing me, "my poor child, why didn't you come to me at once?"

She helped me into her office and made me some tea on her hot plate. She told me I could stay at the school and sleep in the dormitory with the girls who came from the country. She would arrange for me to get a set of false papers.

"Nobody would help me," I told her. "None of my father's friends. Nobody."

"They were afraid," she said.

"Aren't you afraid?"

"Perhaps," she said. "But it is my duty to help you, and that is more important than being afraid. You are my student and have been under my care since you were small. You are also French, and so am I."

Later some of the girls said she took me in because she knew the Germans were losing the war, and that she would be charged with collaborating. But if she could prove that she had hidden a Jewish child then perhaps she could ask for clemency.

I cannot tell. All I know is that she took me in when there was no other place for me to go.

December 1943

THREE WEEKS after it happened, Mme. Sorel came looking for me at school. It was late in the afternoon, and I was working in the study hall, recopying a passage out of Pascal's *Pensées*.

"I want to talk to you," she said. She looked cautiously at the other girls in the room and lowered her voice. "Alone," she said. "Outside."

She raised her eyebrows at me in a significant way, and I understood that she did not trust the other girls. It was hard not to smile. All of them knew what had happened to my family, and that I was hiding at school, using false papers.

Marie and Hélène were smiling at me, and Hélène blew out her cheeks, imitating Mme. Sorel, who was very fat. I came quickly around the table where I was working, took my jacket and followed Mme. Sorel out into the garden.

It had been raining that morning, and there was an icy bite in the air. The stone bench under the wild chestnut tree was too wet to sit on, so we walked around the small garden. As soon as we were outside, Mme. Sorel pulled her scarf tightly around her head, put on her gloves, and started crying. She made a lot of noise, and I was glad there was nobody else to see or hear her. It was just as well that we had come outside because the girls would surely have made funny faces and perhaps even made me laugh.

But here I did not laugh.

"Madame," I said, putting my hand on her arm, "are you all right? Can I bring you some water?"

She shook her head but was still unable to speak. She held on to my arm, and together we continued walking around the garden. I had not taken my hat and my ears began to feel cold. Also, my toes were numb so I stamped my feet several times to warm them up.

Finally she said, "I have a message for you. From your mother."

I stopped walking. "Where is my mother?"

The tears on Mme. Sorel's face seemed to stand still in the cold. She shook her head. "I don't know."

"But you said you had a message from her. Where did you see her?"

"In the Hôtel de Paris. It's where they took all of us. For four days . . ." She began crying again. "And then they took everybody away by train, but they let me go because my brother, Gabriel, came and told them I wasn't Jewish." She rubbed her gloved hand across her face, wiping the tears across her cheeks. Her face was red and chapped. I pulled a handkerchief out of my jacket and handed it to her.

"It wasn't me," she said, gasping and sobbing. "I would have gone with him, but my brother told them, and gave them money. But when this fish-faced German came and asked me was I Jewish, I told him no I wasn't, and neither was Aristide. I told him Aristide converted, that we were married in the church, and that now he was more religious than I. I told him about the holy pictures in the house, and the crucifix over our bed, but he said, 'Your husband is a Jew, and you are lucky we are letting you go.'"

Mme. Sorel wiped her eyes and blew her nose. Then she offered me the handkerchief back. But I didn't want to take it since it was wet from her tears and her nose.

"So they took him away with the others, and they wouldn't let me even see him or say good-bye, or bring him any clothes or food to take with him. You should see what they did to our house—like animals. When I got back I couldn't believe it."

"Yes," I told her, "they did the same at our house."

"They broke the furniture and stole all the silverware, and the radio. They even took the crucifix—it was a beautiful one, silver, that belonged to my grandmother. I should have come to you before, Nicole, because I promised your mother. But I haven't been well, and it took me some time to find out that you were hiding here at school."

"Where are they taking them?" I asked her.

"Who knows? There are prison camps all over France now. France is one big prison camp. To any one of them, I suppose. There is no way of finding out. My brother—he knows the mayor. Nobody knows. We must be patient, and pray that the war ends soon."

"It will," I said. "My father told me, just before it happened, that they were losing. He said the Germans would be driven out of France before the summertime."

"Pray the Good Lord he is right," she said, "and all of us are reunited with our loved ones."

I nodded, and she took my hand and squeezed it.

But I could wait no longer. Not even until the summertime. I had resolved this morning that I would turn myself over to the Germans. I missed my family so much that prison camps no longer held any terrors for me. As long as I was with them, it would be better than it was now.

Day by day my loneliness had grown deeper and harder to bear. For the first few days when I returned to the school, there had been the excitement of being a fugitive, and still the hope that my parents would somehow escape. The hope had gone as the dismal, lonely days became longer. Today, I had resolved during morning class that I would give myself up. It was while Mlle. Reynaud was dictating Pascal's passage that I made the decision.

"Nicole, your mind is wandering again," she said, and added, after inspecting my paper, that my handwriting was even worse than usual, and that I would have to copy the entire passage over again for homework.

I had decided to give myself up. Perhaps today I would go, or tomorrow, or the next day. But I would go. And now, here was Mme. Sorel with a message from my mother. It seemed almost a sign.

"Your mother said," Mme. Sorel was saying, "for you to behave."

I looked down at the ground, and moved my foot back and forth a few times. This message was surely from my mother.

"She said you must eat as much good food as you can get, keep yourself as clean and warm as possible, and not be always talking back to grownups, and thinking that you know best."

I was looking down at my foot, and thinking that it was a good thing I had not received her message before I went to the Durands. Maman would be ashamed of me.

Mme. Sorel was silent.

"Was there anything else?" I asked.

She said nothing, so I looked up. She was crying again, this time silently. I had to wait a few more minutes before she continued.

"There is more," she said. "Your mother said that she loves you very much and has faith that you will always do the right thing."

"She said that?" I stopped looking at my feet.

"Yes, and there was one more thing."

"What was it?"

"That you must not get caught."

I looked down at my feet.

"She said that whatever suffering lies ahead for them, she and your father could bear up as long as they knew you were safe. She said knowing that you were safe would keep them going, and that they would come back to you as soon as they could."

"And . . . ?"

"That's all. Maybe she would have said more but when they let me go everybody wanted me to take a message to somebody or other, and the Germans were all over . . . listening."

She shuddered, and looked over her shoulder. "I feel as if they're listening now. Everywhere I go, I feel as if they are listening."

"And . . . my father?" I asked.

"Your father?"

"Didn't he send me a message too?"

Mme. Sorel blinked, and then put an arm on my shoulder. "But he was not with us. They separated the men and the women."

"Not together?"

She held me in her arms, and offered me the handkerchief. I wiped my eyes and blew my nose. Not together!

After a while, she said, "How are they treating you here, Nicole?"

"Quite well, Madame."

"You know," she said, "I was astonished to hear that you were at the school. Everybody knows that Mlle. Legrand is pro-German. Your family had so many friends. Why did you take such a chance, and come here?"

"Because nobody else would take me."

Mme. Sorel left very soon afterward. She said she would come back and bring me some cheese and maybe some apples and a pair of warm stockings. Her brother had many connections. I never saw her again. She left Aix-les-Bains, and nobody knew where she went.

So I will not give myself up to the Germans. I will wait here at school in Aix-les-Bains for the war to end and my parents to return.

I am sorry now that I gave Françoise my locket with the pictures of Maman and Papa in it. I would like to feel it around my neck, and think that their faces are with me all the time.

I have the picture album. It is the only thing I took from the apartment, and I think it was the best. All of those pictures are so happy. There is one I like more than any of the others. It was taken at the beach, in 1939, before the war started. Papa is seated on a blanket in the sand. There is a large picnic basket next to him. Jacqueline is sitting in his lap, eating a peach. I am kneeling on one side of him, laughing up into his face, and Maman, seated on the other side, is waving and smiling at the camera.

I can see that picture even when I close my eyes. Even when I am in my bed at night. I like to think of that picture, and I tell them when they come to me that soon we will be together again. Soon there will be a day like that day when our family packs a huge picnic lunch in a basket and goes off together to the beach. I know that there will be a day like that, and sometimes, in the darkness here, I can feel the sunshine on my face.

MARILYN SACHS, a native New Yorker, received her Bachelor of Arts degree from Hunter College and a Master's degree in Library Science from Columbia University. As a specialist in children's literature, she was with the Brooklyn Public Library for more than ten years and with the San Francisco Public Library for five years. She now devotes full time to writing and is recognized as an outstanding children's book author. *The Bears' House* was a 1971 nominee in children's books for the National Book Award. *Veronica Ganz* was selected by the American Library Association as one of the Notable Children's Books of 1968.

Mrs. Sachs lives in San Francisco with her husband, Morris, her son, Paul, and her daughter, Anne.

A Pocket Full of Seeds
Marilyn Sachs
Illustrated by Ben F. Stahl

Nicole Nieman is not very different from other girls. She is jealous of her younger sister Jacqueline, doesn't like her teacher, Mlle. Legrand, and often gets mad at her mother, particularly when Maman accuses her of having a big mouth. Nicole has a best friend, whose name is Françoise, but she longs for the friendship of Lucie Fiori who seems to despise her. Like other girls, Nicole enjoys parties, presents, good food, and beautiful dresses.

But unlike most other girls, Nicole's world and even her life is threatened. She lives in France at the time of the German occupation in World War II, and over a period of five years the terror that was spreading across Europe gradually encroaches on Nicole's town. Her family, being Jewish, must escape from the approaching Germans. But where can they go to find safety? Maman says to Switzerland. Papa says they might be shot crossing the border. And Jacqueline cries because she is afraid. In five years, Nicole grows up from a smug little girl of eight to a courageous, resourceful teenager of thirteen, who lives with the possibility that she may never see her family again.

Marilyn Sachs has based A POCKET FULL OF SEEDS on the actual events in the childhood of a friend, and the result is a poignant, extremely touching war story.
even more awards.

Jean Mercier, *Publishers Weekly*

Nous ~~voulons~~ devons reconstruire, ~~et~~ mais la préface nécessaire à ~~toutes~~ cette reconstruction c'est d'éliminer l'individualiste destructeur, destructeur de la famille dont il ~~brise ou~~ relâche les liens — destructeur du travail à l'encontre du quel il proclame le droit à la paresse, ~~destructeur~~ de la Patrie, dont il ébranle la cohésion quand ~~il n'en dissout pas l'unité~~ et sape son unité. Seul le don de soi donne son sens à la vie individuelle. Il la ratache à quelque chose qui la dépasse, qui l'élargit, et la magnifie.

Pour conquérir tout ce que la vie comporte de bonheur et de sécurité, chaque français doit commencer par s'oublier lui-même. Qui est incapable de s'intégrer dans un groupe, d'acquérir le sens vital d'une équipe ne saurai prétendre à servir, c'est à dire à remplir son devoir d'homme et de citoyen. Il n'y a pas de société sans amitié, sans confiance, sans dévouement. Je ne vous demande pas d'abdiquer votre indépendance. Rien n'est plus légitime que la passion que vous en avez. Mais l'indépendance peut parfaitement s'accommoder de la discipline, tandis que l'individualisme tourne inévitablement à l'anarchie et ne trouve d'autre correctif que la tirannie. Le plus sûr moyen d'échapper